THE MATTER OF MANDRAKE

THE MATTER OF MANDRAKE

BARRY NORMAN

BRASH
BOOKS

ISBN-13: 978-1-954841-96-3
Published by
Brash Books
PO Box 8212
Calabasas, CA 91372
www.brash-books.com

For My Mother and Father

TABLE OF CONTENTS

INTRODUCTION

THE MOST AMIABLE OF FICTIONAL HEROES BY MIKE RIPLEY

first met Barry Norman through his wife Diana, who wrote prize-winning historical mysteries under the name *Ariana Franklin*, but of course I had known Barry for more than twenty years as the UK's favorite movie critic thanks to his iconic film review programmes on television. If you were at all interested in movies and wanted to know what was worth watching, then Barry Norman was your spirit guide, describing the latest Hollywood offerings with wit, enthusiasm and always fairness.

In particular, I remember him strongly recommending a new film by a debut director nobody had heard of which was being widely condemned in the British media for its violence and bad language. The film was *Reservoir Dogs* and the director Quentin Tarantino. Legend has it that when the two finally met at the Cannes Film Festival, Tarantino thanked Norman for being the man 'who stood up for *Reservoir Dogs*.'

Not surprisingly, being the son of respected British director Leslie Norman and brought up around actors, producers and film technicians, movies and the film world invariably feature in Barry Norman's books – and why not? When, in the 1960s, he joined the legion of journalists inspired by the success of the James Bond films to try their hand at writing a thriller, it was no surprise that the plot involved the filming of a Biblical epic.

In an interview with *Empire* magazine in 2014, Barry recalled his debut as a novelist in 1967: "The first book I wrote was a thriller called The Matter of Mandrake with a hero who was halfway between Len Deighton's nameless hero and James Bond."

Interviewed by me for *Shots* magazine, Barry recalled meeting Len Deighton for the first time, around 1966 in the journalists' pub The White Swan (known locally as The Mucky Duck) off Fleet Street:

"Personally, though I very much took to the guy, I wasn't all that happy with Len Deighton. At the time I had just written my first spy novel rather in the James Bond genre and I wasn't that chuffed about some bloke coming along and changing the whole business (of spy fiction)."

The Matter of Mandrake is a quintessentially British thriller of the 1960, featuring exotic locations (the British were only just discovering holidays abroad) and lush lifestyles, with plenty of attractive females (often described as 'birds') and very consensual sex, though not in any graphic detail which would only slow down the action. The plot involves a disgraced Government minister and some missing defence plans – both elements all too plausible in that decade.

Mandrake introduced two new features: First, Paul Baker, a hero who is really a journalist and a reluctant amateur in the spy business and does not take himself too seriously and, second, the wonderfully bizarre world of movie-making, in this case a production in dubious taste called *The Life and Loves of Pontius Pilate* being filmed in Madrid.

His father Leslie, then directing television episodes of *The Sain,t* gave the manuscript pre-publication to Roger Moore saying *"There's a movie here and a part for you."* Moore took the book on holiday, read it, and on his return agreed to the idea of film with Norman Senior directing and Norman Junior trying his hand at scriptwriting, but it was not to be. Moore found himself committed to a further fifty-seven episodes of *The Saint* and, once free of that, chose to play James Bond rather than Paul Baker.

The novel received good reviews in England, *The Observer* calling it a "very lively and readable ultra-sexy spy thriller" and the *London Evening Standard* picked up on its "Polished thrills, energetic action and some hilarious comedy."

The book is shot through with Barry Norman's off-the-cuff witticism, especially when dealing with move people, and his hero Paul Baker seems almost apologetic about the way in which females throw themselves at him, not to mention the ridiculousness of being asked to carry two baby Browning pistols, one of them in his underwear (making a quick draw both difficult and embarrassing). In many ways, Baker is the soul-mate of that other Sixties sham-hero, John Gardners' Boysie Oakes a.k.a. *The Liquidator*, but Baker is not as cowardly and has a real, empathetic romantic streak as he showed in his second outing in *The Hounds of Sparta* in 1968.

Once again, Baker is called upon by the enigmatic Mr. Chatham, who runs a shady off-the-books section of the security service, this time to go to the island of Crete where a washed-up alcoholic agent thinks he has stumbled on a Soviet plan to assassinate a vacationing British scientist in line for a key job in germ warfare research. Picking up an official 'assistant' (a very liberated female of course) in Greece, Baker's arrival in Crete sees the very undignified death of the former agent and an attempt on his own life, but the professor seemingly in good health and fine spirits. In London and then Scotland, Baker has to find out what exactly is going on whilst balancing his love life and he has to survive a very close encounter with a Russian submarine!

Sadly, for Baker was the most amiable of fictional heroes, he featured in only the two novels. Barry Norman went on to write other novels, memoirs and many books on films and film stars (ad cricket, another passion of his), but only returned to the thriller proper in 1992 with *The Birddog Tapes* and then *The Butterfly Tattoo* (published in the UK as *The Mickey Mouse Affair*).

In this pair of novels, Norman abandoned the themes of spies and espionage and created a new hero, Bobby Lennox, to provide an undeniably British take on the hardboiled private eye tale.

Bobby Lennox is a boxer who never quite made it, who became involved with the London underworld in his youth and gets himself an (almost) accidental reputation as a hit-man. In *The Birddog Tapes*, ghosts from his past lead him to Hollywood (where he tries, hilariously, to pass himself off as Michael Caine!) ostensibly on a contract as a hitman, the only problem being he knows the intended victim very well indeed. Then the man taking out the contract is himself murdered and Lennox finds himself in web of blackmail. No less than Elmore Leonard said: "A thriller set in Hollywood today. This is good stuff."

In *The Butterfly Tattoo*, Lennox again finds himself tackling a case of blackmail, this time of a British government minister by the anonymous 'Mickey Mouse' in a Walt Disney-inspired criminal gang. In the UK, the novel was originally titled *The Mickey Mouse Affair*.

In both cases, Lennox proves to be a resourceful, deceptively tough protagonist with a strong core of humane sensitivity and he, like Paul Baker, benefits hugely from Barry Norman's instinctive wit and self-depreciating style.

Mike Ripley is the author of more than thirty books and has reviewed over 950 mysteries for UK newspapers and magazines. He is known as the unofficial historian of British thrillers.

CHAPTER ONE

A SIN OF COMMISSION

"I SIMPLY DON'T understand you," said Jarvis Charterhouse. He pronounced it Charteris, because he was that kind of man. If he had not been called Charterhouse, pronounced Charteris, he would probably have been called Cholmondely, pronounced Chumley. And even if he had been called Smith, he would have pronounced it Smythe. "I really don't. I think you must be mad."

"Oh well," said Paul Baker, with a small, non-committal shrug. He did not feel qualified to argue the point. Charterhouse was, after all, his agent and the great thing about agents, surely, was that they always knew best.

"I mean, how much are you getting for this job—twenty quid, is it?"

"Twenty-five," Paul said, defensively.

"Well, there you are." From a thick, squat cigarette case Charterhouse took a thick, squat cigarette of a kind made specially for him by one of those old-world, carriage-trade firms in Jermyn Street and which he never, on any account, offered to anyone else. He lit it with a Zippo which was saved from complete ordinariness by the fact that his initials were engraved upon it in gold.

From the topmost strand of his sleek, superbly cut grey hair to the glistening tips of his elastic-sided shoes, taking in *en route* the mid-grey Savile Row suit, the white silk shirt and the black, knitted silk tie, he was an astonishingly smooth man; so smooth that, unless in his presence, Paul often wondered whether he really existed.

"It's done now, anyway," Paul said. "I couldn't back out if I wanted to."

"I understand that. What I don't understand is why. Are you hard up or something?"

"Not especially."

"Then you must be mad. It's the only answer." Charterhouse swivelled his chair right round so that he was staring at the bare, pearl-grey wall behind him and presenting only his elegant back to Paul's gaze.

Charterhouse did this to all his clients when he wished to show displeasure. In an age when every other man was an agent of some kind, even literary agents—even very good literary agents, which Charterhouse undoubtedly was—needed a gimmick and this was his.

He was famous for it. "Charterhouse turned his back on me again today," eminent authors would remark with casual pride when they met each other at Foyles' Literary Luncheons. "It's the fourth time he's done it."

It had never happened before to Paul and he found it rather impressive. He was also flattered for he was small-time as Charterhouse's clients went and the gimmick was normally reserved for the famous.

A longish period of silence ensued while Charterhouse looked at the wall and Paul looked at the splendidly-tailored back, trying hard to keep his eyes away from the little flecks of dandruff that disfigured his agent's shoulders. They were a mistake, he felt. They should not be there at all and it was almost disloyal of him even to notice them.

The reason for the current exhibition of displeasure was a commission Paul had accepted to go to Spain and write some show business articles for the *Sunday Journal*. Charterhouse believed the price Paul had agreed to was far too low and he was angry about it. He was even more angry about the fact that the entire deal had been made without any reference to himself. This he regarded as a most dangerous precedent.

"You realise, I suppose," he said at length, "that I could have got you a lot more? Fifty at least."

"I don't want any more," Paul said. "I'm quite happy with twenty-five. Besides, I doubt if even you could have pushed the price up. The *Journal* is run on a very tight budget, you know."

"Not all that tight."

Paul sighed and looked for another line of appeasement. "I'm sorry I didn't let you know about it, but it happened quite hurriedly and I had to make a pretty quick decision. Besides, it all seemed rather handy.

"The *Journal* is giving me twenty-five quid, and the film company is flying me over to Madrid and putting me up for a few days. So it won't cost me anything. Added to which, I'll have a return ticket with an open date and, well, it occurred to me that when I'd done the newspaper articles I could shove off to the Costa Brava or something for a few weeks and do some work on my book."

"Oh, yes?" said Charterhouse. He was still not mollified enough to turn round, though.

"At the same time," Paul continued, picking his words with care now that he felt he was near to making a breakthrough, "I thought I might do a couple of travel articles, which you could place with the glossy magazines."

"Aha," Charterhouse swivelled round again at last. Paul felt a small glow of triumph. "That's what I call good thinking. Now, let's see … By the time you get back, say a month from now, the glossies will be planning their new year editions and the holiday supplements. *Luxury* Magazine was very pleased with your sluff on Yugoslavia last year. They'd probably bite again. Then there's *Metropolis* … Oh, yes I think we can turn this little trip of yours to good account, after all."

"Fine," said Paul, pleased that they were friends again.

"Mind you," Charterhouse waved a long, pale hand in warning, "the fact remains that you should never have accepted the original commission without talking to me first. It was very bad of you."

Paul said nothing but looked contrite. It seemed to be enough; and they began to talk in a business-like way about the travel articles he would write.

When they had finished, Charterhouse rang for his secretary and ordered tea. It came, in astonishingly quick time, in blue wedgwood cups; or rather, in a blue wedgwood teapot. Charterhouse himself poured it into the cups.

"You puzzle me, Paul." He said, "I hope you don't mind my mentioning it?"

"Not a bit. What puzzles you?"

Charterhouse lit another of his squat cigarettes and Paul, after waiting vainly to see if he was to be offered one now that the atmosphere was so chummy, lit one of his own—a brand specially made for him and a few million other people by Players.

"Do you know how much you earned last year?" Charterhouse asked. "Five hundred and forty-seven pounds. Plus a few shillings. I happened to look it up just before you called in."

"Really," said Paul. "Not much, is it?"

"No, it's not. And it isn't as if you couldn't earn more. You could do very well, you know, with your travel stuff. I mean, you only worked about three months last year."

"I felt lazy," said Paul.

Charterhouse poured himself another cup of tea. "It's none of my business, of course, but I do sometimes wonder how you manage to live. You obviously don't do it on five hundred a year. Your flat must cost you more than that. And then you don't live badly."

"To tell you the truth," said Paul, "I go about robbing banks." He was enjoying this—the eager curiosity, the unsubtle inquisition and the other man's slight but obvious embarrassment.

"Private means, I suppose," Charterhouse ignored the crack about robbing banks. "You're a lucky chap."

"Yes. I had this old auntie," Paul said. "Very fond of me, she was, so when she died she left the lot to me and since she was pretty well-heeled it means I have quite a nice income." He often felt rather guilty about the money, suffering a superstitious sort of fear that an income so casually and luckily acquired could not really be a good thing. Such feelings, he had decided, stemmed from his Puritan ancestors and went along with his inner convictions, usually firmly suppressed, that happiness had to be paid for and that enjoyment was morally bad for one. He drew solace from the fact that he was not alone in these fears, that the English as a race were very much prey to them, which among other things, explained why they were frequently so uneasy about sex.

"Wish I had an old auntie," said Charterhouse. "I'd be out of this game like a shot if someone left me some money."

This, as they both knew, was simply not true. Charterhouse was a born agent. If agents had never existed, he would have found it necessary to invent them.

They finished their tea and their cigarettes and Paul got up to go.

"When are you off?" Charterhouse asked, escorting him to the door.

"Tomorrow morning."

"Have a good trip. You should do. Nice time of year to see Spain. Send us a postcard. And work hard on those travel articles."

They shook hands.

"Oh, by the way, how's the book going?" Charterhouse was merely being polite. He was not very interested in the book. Unless, by some miracle, it turned out to be a best seller there would be little in it for Paul and even less for himself.

"Okay. I should finish it before the winter." A likely tale, Paul thought, as he ran down the dark, narrow little stairway. He had hardly got beyond the first chapter. Still, one day, when he found time …

He walked across the road and waited in the queue for a bus to Knightsbridge. In the glass door of a shop, he caught a glimpse of his own reflection. Dark hair, cut in the currently fashionable style, which meant short and neat and brushed slightly forward. Blue eyes. Cruel blue eyes, he sometimes deluded himself into thinking. He wore a black sports coat with an unostentatious white fleck, dark grey slacks, narrow, with cross-pockets and no turn-ups, the inevitable elastic-sided shoes of the period and a black, knitted tie. Not silk, like Charterhouse's. Terylene.

The whole effect, crisply set off by a white shirt with a tab collar, was a little sombre but rather smart. He looked like a comfortably successful young journalist, which he was and which, at this time more than any other, was precisely how he wanted to look.

When the bus dropped him at the top of Sloane Street he walked briskly to his flat in one of the fashionable little squares that abound in the area. As flats went, it was nothing particularly remarkable, though an estate agent would have been justified in calling it desirable. Indeed, an estate agent had called it desirable, which was how Paul had come to find it in the first place.

He mixed a whisky and dry ginger, lit a cigarette, removed his jacket and made a phone call to a Whitehall number. When he got the extension he wanted, he said, "Baker here. All set. I'm off tomorrow."

The man at the other end said: "Right, good luck." And then hung up.

Paul finished his cigarette and started packing for the next day's trip. A dark, lightweight suit for evening wear, a blue sports coat and matching slacks, several shirts, ties, socks, underwear and pyjamas.

In the small hand-grip in which he carried his professional equipment, he put a wad of copy paper, two notebooks, and a spare typewriter ribbon, leaving enough room for the carton of duty free cigarettes and the bottle of duty free Scotch he would collect on the plane.

By the time he had finished, he had packed the usual paraphernalia of a journalist setting off on an assignment abroad. It was all quite unremarkable—except for two things.

Two automatics.

They were both Browning 0.25s, quite tiny—four and a half inches by three inches.

One, in a shoulder holster, he slipped underneath his typewriter in its metal case.

The other, small, shiny and cold, nasty as a black beetle, he regarded distastefully for a moment. Then he undid his trousers and put the little gun into a pouch pocket that hung down inside, suspended by short straps from two buttons on his waistband.

It was not exactly the kind of place from which a quick draw was possible. In fact, there was only one way to get the pistol out—the same way as he had put it in. And since this meant unfastening his trousers he would be likely to find himself extremely embarrassed if he were ever called upon to draw a gun upon some latter-day Mata Hari.

The only advantage of keeping a gun there at all was that it was possibly the last place anybody would expect to find one.

He zipped up his trousers and looked down at himself. The bulge the gun made was very slight. It was hardly noticeable even now and, with a jacket buttoned over it, would be completely hidden.

Paul grinned wryly and went to pour himself another drink. The gun lay hard and uncomfortable against the flat of his stomach and he felt both slightly ridiculous and, because he was not used to guns, uneasy.

CHAPTER TWO

FLASHBACK I

THE ROOM was small and cheerless, furnished with the bare minimum of bits and pieces. There was a table and a couple of chairs, an old TV set with a 12-inch screen, a nondescript cupboard and a stretch of grimy, brown lino on the floor. A naked light bulb, hanging motionless from the centre of the ceiling, threw a bitter unfriendly light into every corner, and shone with particular cruelty on the man who sat beneath it on a hardbacked kitchen chair.

He was just a little man, middle-aged and bald, and he leaned heavily forward, kept from falling by the heavy thongs that bound his ankles and wrists to the chair.

He had obviously suffered and he was suffering still. His nose, which once had been an ordinary sort of nose, a little bulbous but otherwise unremarkable, now spread, shapeless and broken, across his face. His eyes were cut and swollen and already the angry red of the skin around them was turning to shades of blue and purple and green.

At first he had shouted, screamed, calling in his despair for help. But he had given that up a long time ago. No help had come and he knew that no help would ever come, for there was nobody to hear him. In this dreary, shabby house he was all alone.

All alone … except for the man, the big man who lounged before him now, comfortably at ease in the room's one armchair, reading a late edition of the *Evening Standard* and tutting quietly over the surprise transfer of Fulham's right-back to Tottenham Hotspur.

The man who had been waiting in the dark when the other came home so unsuspectingly. The man who had hit him hard on the back of the neck with a vicious little rubber cosh; who had tied him to the chair and waited for him to regain consciousness.

The man who had then plied him with questions and, when he gave the wrong answers or refused to answer at all, had beaten him and questioned him again, then beaten him until consciousness came and went and the little man lost all track of time and was aware only of pain.

He tried now to struggle upright in the chair and the movement forced a thin wail of agony through the bruised tyres of his lips. At the sound the big man put down his paper and glanced over at his victim.

"Ah," he said. "You're with me again." He sounded pleased. He had the cosh in his hand and he stood in front of the little man, flexing his wrist ready for action.

"Where had we got to?" he said. The little man offered no reply and received a smart crack across the ribs for his insolence.

"Listen to me," the big man said. "How much do your people know about Madrid? Eh?" He was shouting now, as if the little man was old and deaf and senile. "How much do they know about Pontius Pilate?"

His victim slumped forward again and he pushed him back upright in the chair. "Look, I don't want to be too hard on you. Just give me a straight yes or no. All right?"

Another bit of efficient work with the cosh. Then, at last, the little man surrendered; weakly, as if the effort was almost unbearable, he nodded.

"Good man. Now then. Do your people know about Madrid?"

A pause that stretched into many slow seconds. The big man gripped the cosh more tightly and drew his arm back, his wrist loose to give the maximum follow-through. He was quite an artist in his own field.

Then … "Yes." It was almost inaudible, thick and guttural; a sound that seemed to have come from far, far away.

"They do?" The big man frowned. "Are you sure?"

"Yes."

"That's not so good," he said, softly, to himself. Then, louder: "What about Pontius Pilate? Do they know about that?"

This time the pause was even longer but the big man hesitated to use the cosh again. A waxen look was coming over the little man's face and his breathing was dangerously faint. After a while his eyes opened and he looked up, squinting in the light of the bulb.

"Yes," he said. "They do." It was the last thing he ever said and it was a lie. But as he drifted off into an unconsciousness from which he would never recover, he felt good about it. In a curious way, he felt that he had won and the big man had lost.

"Hmm." The big man watched him for a moment. Then from his pocket he took a small pistol and placed the muzzle hard against the left side of the little man's chest.

He hesitated just for a second, contemplating the consequences of the action he was about to take. Then he shrugged and the gun bucked a little in his hand as he squeezed the trigger.

CHAPTER THREE

FLASHBACK II

A T PRECISELY 10 a.m. the next day, the little man, whose name was Hector Neece, had been due to make a phone call to a Mr. Chatham in Whitehall. The call was never made.

Mr. Chatham at first was somewhat perturbed, but not unduly so. Men in Neece's line of employment were not always punctual. They tended to be, Mr. Chatham thought with faint disapproval, a little irregular.

He went about his other business and waited. But by 10.30 he was becoming anxious and at 11 he was definitely worried. The call he had been expecting was no routine affair. It was important, vitally so. Not exactly a matter of life and death—and even if it had been, Mr. Chatham would never have allowed so melodramatic a phrase to stray into his mind. Still, it was a matter of urgency and so, at 11.15, he did what people in Whitehall frequently do and set the appropriate machinery in motion.

One hour later, a man wearing a Burton's suit and carrying a suitcase walked briskly into a rather nasty, decaying house in Islington and went up to the top floor.

There was nobody around to challenge him for the house was under demolition order and only the top floor was still occupied. But if someone had appeared and asked his business he would have declared himself a travelling salesman and opened his suitcase to prove it. The case was filled with a dozen or so samples of ladies' cheap underwear—or, as he sometimes put it drolly to himself, cheap ladies' underwear. He had been carrying it around for nearly ten years and had never sold so much as a pair of pants to anyone.

He trod lightly on the stairs, his rubber-soled shoes making hardly any noise and when he reached the top landing, he put his case down and listened for a full minute. There was no sound from anywhere within the house. Satisfied, he went to the door facing him and opened it with a key which he selected from a bunch that he carried in his jacket pocket. When the lock clicked, he flung the door open and waited again, pressed against the landing wall. There was a revolver in his hand.

Nothing moved. Nothing happened.

He went into the room and stopped, staring at the crumpled little body that still sat slumped forward, wrists and ankles tied, in the upright chair. A look of pain passed briefly across the salesman's face. Then he went out, shutting and locking the door behind him, and ran downstairs to the public telephone box across the road.

He spoke briefly on the phone and went back upstairs to wait.

In less than half an hour an ambulance drew up outside and four men in uniform came up the stairs to the top floor. Two of them removed the body from the chair, laid it on the stretcher they had brought for the purpose and covered it with a white sheet. After which they sat down quietly and smoked cigarettes while the other two and the travelling salesman searched the room with rapid but methodical precision.

"Why does it need four of you?" the salesman asked irritably.

"Union rules," said one of the smokers, not looking up.

"Very funny."

None of them spoke again until the salesman grunted and said: "This looks interesting." It was a sheet of paper which he had discovered in the back of a drawer, partly covered by shirts and rolled-up pairs of socks.

He read what was written upon it shrugged and put it away in his pocket. If the little man had been around to watch he would have felt even better about the last lie he ever told. For the discovery of the piece of paper meant that it was not a lie at all.

The salesman glanced round the room. The others had finished their jobs and were waiting for him.

"All right," he said. "Let's go."

CHAPTER FOUR

FLASHBACK III

A T AROUND one o'clock in the afternoon on the day after Hector Neece's body was discovered, Paul Baker, who had been to a cocktail party given by an American air line, left the Ballroom entrance of the Dorchester Hotel and stood on the kerbside in Park Lane, staring up towards Marble Arch in the somewhat forlorn hope of finding a taxi.

The only problem on his mind was whether he had really succeeded in talking the vice-president of the airline into giving him a free flight to Los Angeles in return for a favourable mention in the articles Paul would subsequently write. Paul doubted it somehow. It was the kind of proposition vice-presidents of airlines turned down every day with less thought than they would give to declining a second large brandy after lunch.

Still, it had been worth a try and it might work yet. Thus preoccupied with these thoughts and the necessity for keeping a sharp look-out for a cab, he hardly noticed the dark saloon car that stood at the kerbside outside the Ballroom. Nor did he notice the two men in sober suits who got out of the car, until they stopped, one on either side of him.

"Excuse me, sir. Are you Mr. Paul Baker?" The question was put by the younger of the men.

"Yes. I am."

"Do you mind telling us your address?" asked the older man.

"What?" Paul looked at them suspiciously. "Are you from *Candid Camera* or something?"

"No. Would we be right in thinking you live at number 25 Gorleston Square, SWI?"

"No, you wouldn't. I live at 17a."

The younger man looked at his companion and nodded.

"Good," said the older of the two. "Would you mind coming with us, sir?"

"Why?"

"You could call it official business."

"You're from the police?"

"Not exactly."

"Oh my," Paul said. "Very cloak and dagger, aren't we? Which of you is James Bond?"

"Another comedian." The younger man sighed. "Are you coming with us?"

"Do I have a choice?"

"Yes."

"All right, then. Just so long as I have the choice I'll come."

The three of them got into the car, the younger man driving, and set off down to Hyde Park Corner, into the park, past Buckingham Palace and down the Mall towards Whitehall.

"Come on," Paul said. "You can trust me. What's it all about?"

But neither of them answered him and they carried on in silence until they pulled up in the courtyard of a tall building not far from the Thames Embankment. Paul recognised it as an annexe to the Board of Trade.

"I know this place," he said. "My father used to work here."

Still neither of the men replied and, with a sigh, he followed them through a side entrance, into a lift and up to the third floor. The corridor into which they emerged was as undistinguished as any other corridor in any other Whitehall office block. At this time of day it was deserted and no sound came from behind the closed doors as they passed.

About two-thirds of the way down, the younger man stopped at a door that was simply marked Private, knocked, opened it and put his head inside.

"Mr. Baker is here, sir," he said.

"Send him in."

The two men stood aside and Paul was ushered in and the door was closed softly behind him.

The room he found himself in had a drab, Ministry of Works carpet on the floor and drab Ministry of Works paint on the walls. It also had a few filing cabinets, a couple of chairs and a desk. Behind the desk was a tall, thin, elderly man with a stoop and rimless spectacles. He had dry, yellowing skin—the result, Paul supposed, of having knocked about in the tropics—a dry hand-shake and a dry voice. His clothes were formal and so was his manner.

"Please sit down. Mr. Baker."

Paul sat down and waited. He would have lit a cigarette had it not been for the fact that the latest lung cancer death figures were prominently displayed on the wall behind the desk. Paul could take a hint. He left his cigarette case in his pocket and contented himself with biting absent-mindedly at a finger nail.

"My name is Chatham," said the dry man. "Your father was a colleague of mine. He was a very able man."

Paul inclined his head in acknowledgement. His father had died eight years ago and Paul was always pleased to hear him praised. "It's because of that," said Mr. Chatham, "that I wanted to see you."

"The invitation," Paul said, "could have been a little more orthodox."

"Yes, I appreciate that. Unfortunately, it was a matter of some urgency and though I don't usually approve of these … ah …"

"Cloak and dagger methods?" Paul suggested, feeling that a useful phrase should not be abandoned simply because it had been used before.

"Precisely. Although, as I say, I don't usually approve of such methods, I felt that in this case they might save an appreciable amount of time."

"No doubt about that," Paul said. It was barely twenty minutes since he left the Dorchester.

Mr. Chatham cleared his throat with a sound like a chair scraping on linoleum and said: "I shall come straight to the point. I had you brought here, because I should like you to undertake a task which could, melodramatic though it may sound, be of some importance to this country. What I should like to know first is whether you are, in principle, free and willing to undertake such a task."

He paused enquiringly and Paul said: "Is it dangerous?"

"No. I would say not at all."

Mr. Chatham paused again and stared with some distaste at the carpet. Paul, both intrigued and bewildered, said: "I'd like to hear more. But I am, in principle, both free and willing."

"Very well. Do you recall the matter of Henry Mandrake?"

Paul nodded. He did indeed. It had been a famous scandal, almost rivalling the Profumo affair in public interest.

Henry Mandrake had been a Cabinet Minister, the first incumbent of a new post—the Ministry of Forward Planning—which had not only a vague title but also an elusive term of reference.

It had never been made quite clear exactly what the Ministry forward-planned, although there had been rumours enough, some of them highly dramatic. And this, combined with the fact that the Minister was youngish, good-looking and unmarried, made Mandrake, as far as the public was concerned, a thoroughly romantic figure.

But one evening, during the course of a raid on an expensive but notorious London club, the police found him in the embrace of a long-haired blonde who, on closer inspection, proved to be another man. Neither of these discoveries occasioned any surprise to the police, who had had Mandrake under surveillance for some time.

As a result of the raid and the fact that the long-haired blonde, smartly turning Queen's evidence, accused Mandrake of having assaulted him, the Minister was arrested, tried and briefly jailed. It had made a considerable stir at the time but since then the matter had been largely forgotten and, as far as Paul knew, Mandrake was now living quietly in retirement somewhere, indulging his sexual appetites in blissful anonymity.

"I remember it very well," Paul said. "But I've not heard anything of Mandrake for quite a while."

Mr. Chatham nodded. "He's spent most of his time in Spain since the trial. He has a villa there, down on the coast somewhere." He paused, reflectively, and added: "Of course, we've been keeping an eye on him."

Paul was surprised. "But what's Mandrake got to do with the Board of Trade?"

Mr. Chatham frowned. "I'm sorry?"

"You are the Board of Trade, aren't you? Or, at least connected with the Board of Trade?"

"Oh, I see," Mr. Chatham smiled. "Officially, yes. Unofficially, not at all. That may seem puzzling to you, but … it's rather difficult to explain exactly what this Department does. Indeed, I'm not at all sure I should try. Our work, is, shall I say, unconventional?"

"I see." Paul thought he saw, anyway. "But, about Mandrake. Why have you been watching him? I know there were a lot of wild ideas about his job but I thought that, basically, he was concerned with birth control and food production and sticking council estates in the middle of the Green Belt. That sort of thing."

"So he was. Basically. But his office covered a very wide area, including a certain aspect of atomic development. It was for that reason that we decided to keep him under observation. It seemed to us that a man like that, even if he had not been a risk while in office, might easily become one when he was out of office.

"So we decided to watch him and it seems we were right, for it appears that he has been negotiating to sell information to the Russians."

"Oh." Paul sat up straighter. Now things were getting interesting.

Mr. Chatham focused his attention on the far wall. Like all the other walls it was painted a colour which, if asked, the Ministry of Works would proudly have called eau-de-nil. Mr. Chatham did not appear to like it very much.

"Briefly," he said, "the atomic project in question was a highly secret plan for a new pocket battleship. Nuclear-powered, of course. There's nothing particularly new in that, except that this project—an Anglo-American one, by the way—was quite revolutionary. These ships would be incredibly cheap to build and operate, twice as fast as any similar vessel currently in existence and fully equipped to destroy a city the size of Southampton in about a quarter of an hour."

"Good Lord!" Paul said. "And Mandrake had the plans?"

"Yes. We believe that he knew, or perhaps just suspected, that the police had him under surveillance and that, as a kind of insurance policy, he made photostat copies of the plans a few days before his arrest."

Paul thought about it. "It would be quite a setback for the West, if the Russians could come up with a fleet of ships like that."

"Indeed. It would be quite appalling. However," said Mr. Chatham, comfortably, "there is very little chance of that happening."

"What? But ... you just said ..."

"Ah, you run ahead of me." Mr. Chatham held up a cautionary hand. "The plans are quite useless. The entire project was based on a false premise. Not only would the battleships be about ten times as costly as at first believed, they would also be remarkably slow and cumbersome."

Bewildered, Paul asked: "Does Mandrake know this?"

"He does not. Neither do the Russians. They both believe the idea to be perfectly feasible. The flaw, you see, was only discovered after Mandrake left office."

Paul shook his head. "I don't understand. If the whole scheme is a cock-up, why not let him sell the plans? They can't be any more good to the Russians than they are to us."

Mr. Chatham regarded him sorrowfully. "My dear Baker, you reveal a regrettable ignorance of international diplomacy. Don't you realise that if the Russians *think* we are in a position to build an enormous fleet of these ships, it's just as good as if we actually could build them? The deterrent value is as great either way."

Paul let the idea sink in. He was still confused but he did not like to show it. He said: "Yes. Quite."

"Therefore," said Mr. Chatham, "it is essential that these plans never get into Russian hands. If they did, the Russians would know at once that the whole project was a failure. They would probably find this out much more quickly than we did. It sometimes seems to me that their German scientists are rather better than our German scientists."

His face disintegrated into a mirthless grin. Paul had heard the joke before and thought it was a lot funnier the way Bob Hope said it, but he grinned, too. It seemed only tactful.

He said: "This is all quite fascinating but where do I come in?"

"Ah, yes." Mr. Chatham fumbled around in the top drawer of the desk and produced the sheet of paper which the travelling salesman had found in Neece's room. "What do you make of this?"

It was a publicity hand-out from the Huxter-Magnus Picture Corporation and dealt, ecstatically, with a three million dollar film (all films these days, Paul thought as he read it, seemed to cost three million dollars) called *The Life and Loves of Pontius Pilate*, which was currently in production in Madrid. There was no doubt about the title. It was repeated eight times in six paragraphs.

Studded around, in between the inevitable superlatives— 'dramatic', 'greatest', 'colossal', 'breath-taking'—were notes about the stars, the director, the producer and the shooting schedule. Written on the bottom in ink was "LAP IB 341. September 2." Paul interpreted this, accurately, as London Airport, a flight number and the date. Yesterday's date.

Mr. Chatham said: "That's a Madrid flight, incidentally." Then he asked: "Do you know anything about the Huxter-Magnus Picture Corporation?"

"A little." In his casual wanderings around Fleet Street, Paul had covered the show business beat for a while.

J. J. Huxter, the founder and chief shareholder of the company, was an American who had settled in London, married an English actress of dubious talent and made a fortune from producing a series of quite dreadful but glossy and richly-mounted pictures. They were the kind of films that never got a Press showing but were advertised screechingly on commercial television in whichever area they happened to be playing. It was a policy that seemed to pay off, because Huxter-Magnus made a lot of films, each slightly glossier and slightly worse than the one before. *The Life and Loves of Pontius Pilate* being the latest, would probably turn out to be the glossiest and the worst yet. Paul told Mr. Chatham this.

"Good. Now, from your experience as a newspaperman, who would be likely to have possession of such a document as this?"

"A hand-out?" Well, almost anyone connected with the film. They're chucked about like confetti. But the obvious people are the publicists, the producer and director, a number of journalists, people in the production office and a handful of secretaries."

"I see." Mr. Chatham stroked his chin with one lean forefinger. "That's what I thought. Now the position is this: that document came into the possession of one of our agents, a man named Hector Neece, who had been working on the Mandrake business."

He picked up the hand-out between his finger and thumb, as if it were something filthy. Mr. Chatham disapproved of film publicity. He disapproved of publicity. He disapproved of films.

"In view of all that," he said, "what are your opinions about this ... ah ... information sheet?"

Paul considered the question for a minute or so. "Was your man Neece booked on that flight, I.B. whatever-it-is?"

"He was. He made the booking in Madrid."

"Then," Paul said. "I imagine that when he made it he jotted the details down on the nearest piece of paper that came to hand."

"On a film publicity hand-out? Why should a man like Neece have such a thing in his possession?"

Paul shrugged. "Depends where he made the plane booking. If he did it on the phone from a kiosk he might have found the hand-out there. I've come across funnier things than film hand-outs in telephone kiosks."

"Quite," said Mr. Chatham dryly. He was silent for a little while. Then he said: "The negotiations between Mandrake and the Russians started, as far as we know, a few months ago. They're being handled by a go-between—almost certainly not a professional spy but someone acting on his own behalf purely from financial motives. We're fairly sure of this for several reasons, if it had been a direct deal with Russia the whole thing would have been concluded by now, which is not so. Also, Neece's recent movements indicate that the middle man operates in or from London and again, since Mandrake is no longer here, there's no valid reason why the Russians should use one of their London-based operatives for this transaction.

"Now, Mandrake is in Spain, this film is being made on location in Spain and Neece had possession of this hand-out. Could that mean that the go-between has something to do with the film?"

Paul considered that, too. "It sounds rather remote. I still prefer my earlier theory. It seems more plausible."

Mr. Chatham leaned back and stared at the ceiling, which, as a daring contrast to the eau-de-nil, had been painted white. "Exactly, and that I may say is the opinion I hold."

Paul shuffled uneasily in his chair and, to hell with the lung cancer figures, lit a cigarette.

"Nevertheless," Mr. Chatham said, "the other theory is a possibility, though as you say, a remote one."

He got up from behind the desk and walked over to the window, half his body still in shadow, the sun and light behind him. He looked suddenly eerie, menacing.

"That, at last, is where you come in, Mr. Baker. I should like you to go to Madrid in your capacity as a journalist and write about this film production. While there, I should also like you to act on behalf of this Department."

It took a little while to sink in but when it did Paul said: "Why me?"

"For several reasons. Let me explain. Our first concern is Mandrake. As matters now stand, he is being very adequately watched and his deal with the Russians cannot possibly go through without our knowing about it.

"The go-between, at this stage, is not basically important. Eventually, in any case, Mandrake will lead us to him. On the other hand, if it can be done without straining our resources too far, we would like to discover his identity as soon as possible."

"But why me?" Paul said again.

"I'm coming to that. *If*—and I underline that word—if this publicity hand-out holds more significance than a mere flight number it may be that the go-between is working for the film company. That being so, it would be useful for us to have somebody on hand, somebody with a watertight reason for being there—a film technician or a journalist. I have nobody available with that kind of cover except you."

"But," Paul said, "what do you want me to do exactly? I don't know anything about your kind of work."

"You don't have to. To put it bluntly, your position will be that of an errand boy for our man on the spot. You will be his 'in' on the film unit. He will tell you what to do and what to look for much more explicitly than I can."

Mr. Chatham came back to his desk and sat down again. "Look, Mr. Baker. I don't think there's much you'll be able to do. You're an insurance policy, that's all. I wouldn't, frankly, have wasted one of my own men on the assignment. It's too much of a long shot and, as I said, we're not too worried about the identity of the go-between. If it hadn't been for you, I don't think I'd have sent anybody to Madrid."

"I see." Paul looked for an ashtray and, finding none, stubbed his cigarette out carefully on his shoe and put the butt in his pocket. "For the third time, why me?"

Mr. Chatham scratched thoughtfully at his ear. His fingernails were long and pointed and remarkably white. "The fact that I knew your father and therefore know something about you."

"Is that really enough? You've given me a good deal of classified information. How do you know you can trust me?"

Mr. Chatham's smile was meagre but confident. "Mr. Baker, I know everything about you. I know how much money there is in your bank account, how many suits there are in your wardrobe, the name of the young lady in whose flat you spent last Sunday night."

The smile, having served its turn, was disposed of. "You are not the first amateur, if I may use that expression, to be asked to do this kind of thing. A number of ordinary businessmen, particularly those who travel a good deal, use their eyes and ears on behalf of this and similar departments. It's not romantic work, nor is it usually exciting, but it can sometimes be useful.

"However, when we use an amateur we pick him carefully. Whenever possible, we choose a likely man long before he may be of use—often, in fact, there is never a need to use him—and study him and his habits and his behaviour very carefully. You're a case in point. Because you are your father's son I've long regarded you as the right sort of material. I think you can be trusted."

"Well," Paul said. And then, as an astounding thought struck him: "Do you mean my father used to do this sort of thing—professionally?"

"Indeed. For many years. Later he was my predecessor in the post I now hold."

"Good God, I always thought he was just a Civil Servant."

"So he was, Mr. Baker. So am I." said Mr. Chatham acidly. "That is all we are here. Just Civil Servants, well will you do it?"

Paul made up his mind swiftly. "Yes. Will you make arrangements for me to go to Madrid or shall I?"

"Better, I think, if you did. Isn't it a fairly simple matter for a journalist to obtain an invitation to visit a film location?"

"If you know how to go about it," Paul said. "When I get there, who do I report to?"

"A man named Blake. I'll give you his address before you leave. He is one of our most efficient men and also, by good fortune, he inherited a small business in Madrid, which gives him the perfect cover there. He was the obvious choice for watching Mandrake. Blake will contact you as soon as you arrive. From then on you will do exactly as he tells you. You can make your own arrangements for reporting to him."

"Sounds all right. Should I ever get in touch with you?"

"Not unless it's absolutely essential and there is no possible alternative. Neither eventuality is likely but, as a precaution, I shall give you a telephone number that you may use under such circumstances."

Paul took a deep breath and let it out slowly. He felt a little shaky now that he had finally committed himself.

He said: "I've just thought of something. Why don't you ask your man Neece about this publicity hand-out?"

"That would have been the obvious thing to do. Unfortunately, he was murdered the night before last."

"What!" Paul leapt from his chair. He was horrified. "I thought you said this job wasn't dangerous."

"Nor is it. There's no reason to suppose that Neece's death and that publicity hand-out are connected. If I thought they were, I shouldn't be sending you to Madrid."

"No." Paul sat down, slowly. "No, I suppose not. One other thing, was there any … suspicious person on that flight? I mean, could Neece have booked himself on it because, for instance, the man he thought to be the go-between was on it?"

"Possibly. Unfortunately, we found out about the flight number too late to get anyone on board and the passenger list was unrevealing."

"Hmm." Paul got up. "You'll want me in Spain as soon as possible, I suppose?"

"Yes, indeed."

They shook hands and Paul made for the door. When he was halfway there, Mr. Chatham called him back.

"By the way, I thought you might like these." He delved into one of the drawers of his desk and produced a small case. When he opened it, Paul saw two small automatic pistols, one in a soft suede shoulder holster; the other in a similarly soft suede pouch with two short straps that had button-holes at the top.

"They belonged to your father," Mr. Chatham said.

Paul's affection for his father was joined by admiration. The new picture of that quietly successful Civil Servant as a man who travelled round the world hunting foreign agents and bristling with small arms was rather exciting.

"The tools of the trade, eh?" he said. "Yes, I'd like them very much."

Mr. Chatham put the guns back into the case.

"What's that pouch for?" Paul asked.

"Ah, yes. I'll tell you how that works …"

CHAPTER FIVE

FLASHBACK IV

T HE TWO men who had brought him there were gone by the
time Paul left Mr. Chatham's office and he found his own
way down to the street. Once there, he set about the business of
getting himself invited to Madrid.

He took the Tube from Charing Cross to Blackfriars and
made his way through the narrow alleys behind Fleet Street to
the dingy, grey building that housed the *Sunday Journal.*

There he asked for the features editor, a man named Sandy
Cray, and in a few minutes a uniformed commissionaire with a
chestful of ribbons and an artificial leg escorted him with great
pomp to the editorial department on the second floor, at which
point a copy boy with nicotine-stained fingers and an out-of-date
Beatles haircut took him on to Cray's office.

The features editor was a neat, red-haired Scotsman with
a habit of burying his head in his hands when people talked to
him, as if the effort of bringing his enormous intellect down to
the level of the problems being discussed was physically painful
to him.

He sat now behind a scarred, wooden desk whose surface
was covered with page proofs and photographs. Paul took the
chair opposite.

"What's all this?" he asked.

"Culture, dear boy," Cray said. "A big piece on the new Shakespeare production at Stratford. It needs a quotation for the headline."

He pressed a buzzer on the desk and pushed the page proofs away from him. "What's on your mind, Laddie?"

Paul began to tell him but was interrupted by the opening of the door and the entrance into the room of Cray's secretary, a debby little blonde with an eager, puppy-dog expression.

"Yes, sir," she gasped, in a little-girl voice that was as out-of-date as the copy boy's haircut.

Cray frowned. "I wanted something. What was it? Oh, yes. Get me *Timon of Athens*, will you?"

She hesitated briefly, then, "Yes, sir," she said and went out again.

"New girl," Cray said. "That's why I'm getting the 'sir' bit. In a couple of weeks it'll be 'Sandy'. No real respect, these birds. Anyway, you were saying … ?"

Paul started again. "I've been offered a facility trip to Spain by Huxter-Magnus Pictures." He lit a cigarette, taking his time about it. No point in seeming too eager to sell the idea. "They're making this epic, *The Life and Loves of Pontius Pilate* in Madrid and I thought there might be some good stuff in it."

Cray nodded, peering out through fingers interlaced across his face. "Such as?"

"Well," Paul chose his words with care. The weakness in his case was that the Pontius Pilate production was not exactly the *Journal's* kind of film. Intellectually it was bound to be vulgar and the *Journal* did not like to be connected with vulgarity. As far as the cinema was concerned, it was basically an Ingmar Bergmann kind of newspaper.

"Well," he said again, "I was thinking of something for your magazine section. Something designed round a good display of pictures ..."

"Crumpet?" Cray broke in, his eyes gleaming.

"Naturally." In fact, Paul had been going to suggest some rather more technical stuff but if crumpet was what the *Journal* wanted, then crumpet was what he would give it. He wasn't proud. Nevertheless, he was somewhat surprised by Cray's question.

"That sounds all right," the features editor said. He glanced up. The surprise must have shown on Paul's face, for he added: "It's a new policy here. We don't want pin-up stuff, you understand. Well, you know the kind of pictures we use—arty and lots of shadow, as if they were all taken in the dark."

"And lots of girls?" Paul prompted.

Cray sighed. "It's the chairman, you see. All of a sudden he's gone potty about birds. Well, he's getting on—be eighty soon. I suppose at that age blokes do start getting odd ideas."

Paul said: "The pictures should be no problem. If necessary, I can get a special set taken."

"Good." Cray put his head in his hands once more and stared meditatively at his crotch. He seemed to find it of absorbing interest. "What else do you think you could do?"

"Interviews, perhaps."

Cray shook his head. "Not film star interviews. We don't go for film star interviews unless they're very big names. Or birds with big charlies."

Paul thought about the cast list he had seen on the handout. There did not seem to have been anyone who came into the *Journal's* rather limited field of interest, though, to be fair, the dimensions of the actresses' charlies had not been mentioned and were, therefore, an unknown quantity as yet.

He said: "I was thinking more of the producer, J. J. Huxter. You know, a mickey-taking piece—The Man Who Made A Million Out of Crap. That sort of thing."

Cray got up and leaned his forehead against the wall over the fireplace. This was another thing he did when he was trying to make a decision.

"A profile in depth," he mused, as if speaking secret thoughts aloud. "Sort of erudite and rather disapproving."

"That's it," said Paul.

The features editor banged his head gently against the wall three or four times, then, turning round, he said: "All right. Sounds reasonable. Wouldn't cost us much, would it?" His eyes narrowed in a crafty sort of way. "We can't pay much, you understand. The coffers won't run to it. Twenty all right?"

Twenty was fine. In this case, five would have done. Paul said: "Thirty?"

"Twenty-five."

"Couldn't go a bit higher, I suppose? Say, twenty-eight?"

"Sorry."

"What about expenses then?"

"Within reason."

Paul seemed to be thinking it over. Finally, he said: "Okay. Twenty-five quid and exes within reason."

"Good. Copy by next Thursday at the latest. And about those pictures."

"Yes?"

"Get some good ones. Lots of thigh and charlies but not pornographic."

"Right."

There was a timid knock, the door opened slightly and in came the secretary again, looking flustered.

"I'm awfully sorry, sir, but I can't find a number for him."

Cray eyed her blankly. "What? What are you talking about?"

"Timon, sir. I've looked through all the contact books very carefully but the only correspondent we seem to have in Athens is a man named Photopopoulos."

There was a moment of such deep silence that Paul could hear, quite clearly, the soft whirring of the electric clock on the wall. Then in a voice infinitely weary, Cray said: "Go." She went.

Cray gave a little sigh. "What do you suppose she would have done," he asked, "if I'd wanted *Two Gentlemen of Verona*?"

Paul shook his head, collected his things and made to leave.

Cray said: "Well, not too pornographic."

"Eh?"

"The pictures. Not *too* pornographic. You know?"

So that part of the confidence trick was accomplished. The rest would now be easy.

The publicity man at Huxter-Magnus in charge of the Pontius Pilate epic was called Ned Masters and looked and sounded rather like Cary Grant, which would have been perfectly all right if someone had not told him so. He had been trying to underline the similarity ever since.

Paul, who had once worked with him for a while on the staff of a morning paper and thus knew what to expect, found him in his Wardour Street office more Cary Grant than ever.

The office was small and white with a blue carpet, and the walls were hung with posters and still photographs from previous J. J. Huxter triumphs, the most eye-catching being a garish red and black advertising bill depicting the Return of Genghis Khan. The background showed a variety of gruesome battle scenes, and the foreground was dominated by the vastly magnified face of a well-known American actor wearing an ill-fitting helmet of doubtful origin and trying to look like Genghis Khan on one of his bad days.

Paul stopped and winced as he saw it. "Good God," he said.

Masters, who had greeted him with his Cary Grant smile and his Cary Grant handshake, took him over for a closer look. "Fetching, don't you think?" he enquired. "My idea, as a matter of fact. Did you ever see the film?"

Paul shook his head.

"Pity. One of our very best. Cost three million dollars and got its money back in under a year."

They sat down at the desk, Masters in the swivel chair facing the Genghis Khan poster and Paul in a straight-backed chair facing the window and, across the street, the offices of the Rank Organisation.

"Long time no see," Masters said. "Where've you been hiding yourself?"

"I've been working on a book." It was a useful explanation and satisfied most enquiries. Few people, Paul had discovered, pried any further for fear of exposing themselves to the awful danger of having the entire plot explained to them in minute detail.

Neddy Masters had no intention of taking that risk. "Good," he said. "Well done," and then he said: "So what are you doing now?"

"Freelancing. Odd features for the papers, bits in the glossies. You know. Actually, what I came to see you about is your Pontius Pilate film. The *Sunday Journal* has asked me to do something on it."

"Really?" Masters raised an eyebrow, Cary Grant fashion. "I shouldn't have thought it was their cup of tea."

"Neither should I but they seem very keen."

"Splendid. I'm not complaining. So what exactly can I do for you?"

"I was wondering," Paul said, "if you could fix me up with a facility trip, out to Madrid."

Masters spread his hands in a gesture of generosity. "Nothing simpler, my dear chap. Matter of fact, we're sending a couple of Fleet Street people out the day after tomorrow. I'll book you on the same flight."

Paul felt a premonitory tingle of excitement. Assuming, as now he must, or what was he doing here anyway? that the go-between in the Mandrake affair had something to do with the Pontius Pilate film, any journalists interesting themselves in that film must be suspect, particularly journalists going to Spain about now.

For if the hand-out was significant, then surely the flight number and date that were written on it must be significant too. They must mean, if nothing else, that the deal between Mandrake and the Russians had not yet taken place, for Neece, the man who had been killed, had booked himself on that flight and surely he would not have planned to reach Spain after the negotiations had been completed.

Casually, Paul asked: "Who are they?"

"Larry Grainger of the *Daily Call* and some columnist from one of the women's magazines. They haven't let us know who they're sending yet. I expect you know Larry, though."

"No. I've never run across him."

"Not a bad chap. Great one for the birds."

Masters glanced at his watch and Paul taking the hint, rose. Masters got up to escort him to the door, one hand resting in the meaningless intimacy of Wardour Street on Paul's shoulder.

"Let's have a drink sometime," Paul said.

Masters threw open the door. "Nothing easier. We'll have one in Madrid. I'm going over there tonight."

And that, Paul thought grimly as he stood in the passage, waiting for the lift, stretched the suspect list to three. Larry Grainger of the *Daily Call*. An unknown columnist from a woman's magazine. And Neddy Masters.

And what's more, he thought further as the lift took him down to street level, I haven't even left the bloody country yet …

CHAPTER SIX

THE GIRL ON THE PLANE

THE CARAVELLE taxied down the runway and stopped, gathering strength for the take-off. The roar of its jet engines grew louder, as if the entire plane was about to disintegrate in one almighty explosion.

Then it was off again, bumping and snarling along the tarmac before making its sudden, surprisingly steep climb towards the cloudless blue of the sky.

The Spanish stewardess said in her heavily accented English: "You may unfasten your seat belts now and you may smoke. Cigarettes only, please, gentlemen."

The girl in the window seat already had her belt unfastened. Paul waited a couple of minutes before undoing his. You never knew, was what he always said. He never liked to unfasten his belt until he was quite certain that the pilot was not going to take it into his head to nip back smartly for something he had forgotten.

He got out his cigarettes and glanced at the girl out of the corner of his eye. She had taken her seat before he got on the plane and, since she was partly turned away from him and towards the window, he had not yet seen her face. All he could see now was the wing of glossy black hair that lay against her cheek.

He held out the cigarette packet towards her and cleared his throat. The girl glanced up from the book she was reading and stared at him uncomprehendingly. Then she noticed the cigarettes and shook her head.

"No, thank you." She went back to her book.

Paul lit up, his hand shaking. She was quite, quite beautiful. In that brief moment when she had gazed at him her looks had impressed themselves indelibly on his mind. Blue eyes, he noted, and searched around for adjectives to describe them. He found none that were worthy. Tanned, smooth skin. A small, straight nose. A wide, full mouth and little, even, white teeth. Never had he seen anything quite so gorgeous.

It became vitally important to know more about her and, in particular, where she was going.

"Madrid?" he asked, all of a sudden. He had not meant to say that. What he had been meaning to say was something quite casual and urbane, witty and sophisticated; something to make her close her book and look up in delighted surprise at finding someone so fascinating in the chair beside her. Instead, he just blurted out "Madrid?" and, said like that with neither preface nor epilogue, it sounded ridiculous.

"What?" She looked up, a little frown making two tiny clefts between her eyebrows.

"I said are you going to Madrid?" A fatuous grin insisted on plastering itself all over his face, so that he was beaming at her like some genial half-wit.

"That's where the plane is going, isn't it?" Her voice was low and nicely controlled; a voice that could, he had no doubt, be soft and warm and purry as a kitten. Right now, though, it had icicles on it.

She returned once more to the book without waiting for an answer, and edged herself a little closer to the window.

Gradually the flush of embarrassment faded from Paul's cheeks. Slightly deflated but by no means undeterred, he puffed at his cigarette and pretended to read the *Daily Mail* while he planned the next stage of his campaign to win her attention.

But before he embarked upon it there was something else he had to do and the urgency of this was brought to his attention by a sharp, stabbing pain in his bladder. He leapt up briskly to show the girl that, even if his conversation was not all that inspired, he was at least a graceful and agile sort of fellow—and remembered, too late, that he had not unfastened his seat belt.

The strong, unyielding material snapped into his stomach and hurled him back against his seat with the force of a catapult.

"Aagh!" he yelped and every eye in the compartment turned to look at him.

"Oh, God," said the girl.

Paul wrenched the belt undone and fled down the aisle to the toilet.

It was ten minutes before he dared to come out and then his fellow passengers regarded him with curiosity, not unmixed with the smug self-satisfaction of people who, feeling perfectly at ease themselves, believe that someone else has just been airsick. He hated them all.

In particular, he hated a smirking young man who lay back in his chair with his feet stuck out in the aisle and said: "First flight, old boy?"

By the time Paul got back to his seat the only person on the plane he did not hate was the girl. And he even had his doubts about her when she murmured, coldly: "I hope you aren't going to be sick on me."

It was too much.

"Now look," said Paul, his voice climbing high with anger. "I have not been sick. I am never sick on aeroplanes. I never will be sick on aeroplanes."

She looked him over, disdainfully. "What were you groaning for, then?"

"I did not groan," he said, pronouncing each word with the very deliberate care of a man who was about to part company with his temper. "The noise I made was an exclamation of surprise. It so happened, if it's any of your business, which I doubt, that I tried to stand up without realising that I hadn't undone my bloody seat belt."

Quite suddenly she started to giggle. "I thought," she said, "that you were about to throw up."

"Charming," said Paul. Sulkily, he turned back to his paper.

After a while he felt her hand on his sleeve and when he looked up she said, in a demure little voice: "May I have that cigarette now, please?"

This time it was his turn to give out the bleak stare—but it was hard to maintain. Despite himself he grinned and she grinned back.

He handed her a cigarette and lit it for her.

"Thanks," she said. She blew smoke in a delicate stream towards the air vent above her head. "My name's Emma Dane," she said.

"Paul Baker." They shook hands.

"Are you going to Madrid, too?" she asked. And then before he could answer, she added hurriedly: "All right, I know. That's where the plane's going, isn't it?"

"Exactly."

"I'm sorry about all that," she said. "I thought you were trying to pick me up."

"I was."

"Oh."

There was a pause ...

"Shall we go back to square one?" Paul asked. "You were sitting against the window, reading a book, and I was looking at a paper. If you like, we can pretend that everything since then never happened."

She thought about it for a while. Her head rested against the crisp white cloth on the seat back as she stared, reflectively, at the cabin ceiling. Paul stared reflectively at her, admiring the striking and unusual combination of the black hair and the blue eyes. Irish blood there somewhere, he thought. She was wearing a light woollen suit in a colour which a couturier would have described as crushed strawberry, or something equally fatuous, and she looked soft and warm and cuddly.

"On the whole," she said, at last, "I think I'd rather be picked up."

From that point they chatted happily but unrevealingly while the steward kept them liberally supplied with champagne and brought, and later removed, their lunch trays. They ate little of the rather plastic food but drank a lot of the champagne.

It was not until the flight was nearing its end that Paul asked: "Incidentally, what are you going to do in Madrid?"

"Well, as a matter of fact," she said, "I'm going out on a film location. I'm a journalist. On one of the women's magazines. *Witch.* Do you know it?"

"That's odd. I ..." He stopped, as the full meaning of what she had just said struck home. Suddenly she was no longer simply a very lovely girl who happened, by sheer chance to be sitting beside him in an aeroplane. She was a journalist going to Madrid, to the same location, quite obviously, as himself. She was suspect number two, the unnamed columnist whom he had filed away in his mind with the as yet unknown Larry Grainger, and Neddy Masters the publicity man. Nonsense, of course. Impossible to think of her as a spy, even worse, a traitor. And yet he had resolved to trust no one, to take this job with the utmost serious-ness—and what kind of resolution was that, if he was going to break it for every pretty girl he chanced upon?

The whole affair was fantastic—a set of worthless plans; a homosexual Cabinet Minister; and somewhere in the background a shadowy go-between who might, or might not, be involved in a preposterous film about the sex life of Pontius Pilate.

Fantastic. And yet a man had been killed, a fact that intro-duced a nasty note of realism into the fantasy.

Last night, his packing done, Paul had settled down to con-sider his own attitude to the job he had been given. Mr. Chatham had more or less told him he was on a fool's errand, and thinking about it rationally Paul was inclined to agree.

Yet he had managed to persuade himself that maybe Mr. Chatham was wrong. There was no point in doing a job unless you believed in it and he made himself believe in this one.

Which meant—what? That everyone was suspect, to be regarded as a potential enemy unless proved a friend. He felt rather silly even thinking this way and so he packed the automatics.

Their presence, secreted about his person and in his belong-ings, was a reminder that absurd though this whole business seemed to be, it was not quite so absurd as all that. Somebody had already been killed. And Mr. Chatham might, just possibly, be wrong. And besides, if Paul was going to play secret agent he might as well play it in costume, even if he did feel more like Walter Mitty than the spy who came in from the cold.

The girl said: "What's the matter?" She looked puzzled. "Why are you staring at me like that?"

"I'm sorry." He glanced away. Already then it was getting hold of him—a swiftly aroused suspicion, a readiness to distrust even those he wanted most of all to trust. It must have been this, the faint beginnings of doubt, that she had seen and not quite recognised in his eyes. It was very alarming, an aspect of the new Baker that he had not reckoned upon at all.

He said: "It's such a crazy coincidence. I'm going out on a film location, too."

"Not this Pontius Pilate thing?" She looked delighted.

He nodded, smiling.

"Oh, I *am* glad. Hey, you're not a journalist too, are you?"

"Right," he said.

"Who with?" And then she said, excitedly: "You don't by any chance know Larry Grainger, do you?"

Horrifyingly, unexpectedly, jealousy crept up to make a shabby trio with suspicion and distrust. Somewhat coldly, he said: "No. Why do you ask?"

"Oh, nothing. It's just that old Neddy Masters told me Larry Grainger was coming out to Spain, too, and I've always wanted to meet him."

"Why?"

She looked quickly round and bent closer towards him, speaking softly. Her hair brushed against his cheek and the smell of some delicate, pleasantly sexy, scent made the blood start rushing madly about his body.

"They say," she said, "that he sleeps with all the pretty girls he interviews. I know an actress who asked him if this was true and he said no, it wasn't entirely true but he was prepared to make an exception in her case."

"Very witty," Paul said, dryly.

"He didn't though."

"He didn't what?"

"Sleep with her. She said she didn't fancy him. But later on she met two other girls who had gone to bed with him and they said he was hot stuff."

"Charming," Paul said.

"Don't be stuffy. You're jealous because you don't sleep with all the pretty girls you interview."

"Well, neither does he. You just said so."

"But he does sleep with some of them."

"How do you know I don't?"

"Do you?" She looked at him with new interest.

"No."

"Oh."

It was beginning to dawn on Paul that he had had too much to drink. His head was a little whoozy and he could feel an incipient hangover establishing a beachhead just behind his right eye.

She said: "Who are you with then?"

"The *Sunday Journal*. Well, not really, I'm a freelance." Something had gone wrong, he thought as he told her about himself. The mood that had been building up between them had turned a little sour. He wondered why. Because, absurd though it might seem, she could be a spy? Or because of his unreasonable jealousy that she seemed disappointed in him for not being the lecherous Larry Grainger? "I write travel articles normally."

"Really? I can't honestly say I've read any of them. Are you cross?"

"No. Why should I be?" But he knew he was and she knew it, too. "I write for the glossies mostly. And I do a lot of stuff for American magazines."

"I expect that pays very well," she said, politely.

"Yes."

And silence came down. They talked some more before the plane landed at Madrid but the conversation never got beyond being desultory. A polite formality had taken over from the intimacy that they had been creating earlier.

He knew this puzzled her and that she could not understand what had happened. But how could he explain?

His head began to ache and a mood of depression settled upon him.

Neddy Masters, glossily Cary Grant in a tan lightweight suit, was waiting for them beyond the Immigration counter.

"I see you two have met," he said. "Good trip?"

"Fine," Paul said, briefly.

Masters took Emma's hand and covered it with both of his. "Lovely to see you, darling. Come on, let's get you through Customs."

They walked off towards the long room where the Customs men, shabby in their cheap, blue uniforms, were waiting, bored and faintly hostile.

Masters stopped: "God," he said, "I'd completely forgotten. Did you see Larry Grainger?"

The glum look that Emma had been wearing for the last half-hour vanished. "Was he on the plane?" she asked "Paul, isn't that marv …" She hesitated as she caught sight of Paul's expression and turned away from him with a faint shrug. Moody. That was the word for him.

"There he is," said Masters.

The smirking young man who had asked if this was Paul's first flight was coming towards them. It's all I need, Paul thought. It would *have* to be him.

The young man was still smirking. On closer inspection he turned out to be a little shorter than Paul had expected and a little plumper, rounder, in the face.

Paul stood aside as Masters made the introductions and churlishly refused to proffer his hand.

"Oho," said Grainger, whose own hands were full of luggage anyway, "our airsick friend."

"Really?" Masters eyed Paul with interest.

"No. Not really," Paul muttered. "Just a misunderstanding."

But nobody was listening, for Grainger was being introduced to Emma. Was holding her hand far longer than was necessary. Was gazing deep into her eyes. Was practically sending up smoke signals that read, "Your place or mine?"

And Emma? She's lapping it up, Paul thought with disgust.

He wished he had not drunk so much on the plane. He wished he had a glass of champagne now. He wished to God that he had never agreed to this job.

And as he trailed along behind the others while some official, obviously in Master's pay, whipped them smoothly through the Customs, he found only one tiny grain of consolation in the whole lousy business. It would be a positive pleasure to regard Grainger as Suspect Number One.

CHAPTER SEVEN

NO MAN IN MADRID

T HE HOTEL Peniscola (or "Penis Colour" as Neddy Masters insisted on calling it—"You've seen Technicolor. You've seen Warnercolor," he declared as the car pulled up outside. "Now Huxter-Magnus Films are proud to present—Penis Colour." He thought it very funny and laughed a lot.) was a lofty, white, new-ish building which, if nothing else, blended with the other sky-scrapers that were beginning to dominate the Madrid skyline.

It stood about half a mile from the city centre, just off the wide, tree-lined Paseo de la Castellana, and differed from most of the other new hotels in that it had a garden, which sprouted briefly on either side of the building and rather more extensively at the back. Marble steps led up to the huge, plate-glass doors of the main entrance where a dozen pink-uniformed porters divested arriving guests of everything they were not actually wearing and disappeared with their booty into some mysterious sorting office just off the vestibule.

Half an hour after his arrival, Paul was sitting in his bedroom on the second floor, wondering whether he would ever again see the typewriter, the hand-grip and the light raincoat that had been wrested from his grasp as he set foot within the hotel.

He was still feeling depressed. The champagne he had drunk had turned sour on him and his stomach kept reminding him of the fact by sending small jets of bile into his throat.

In addition he was suffering a feeling of let-down leavened with anxiety. Blake had not been at the hotel to meet him, had not, in fact, even left a message and Paul was already beginning to wonder whether something had gone wrong.

The result of all this was that even the hospitality of Huxter-Magnus, which was on an almost ostentatious level, failed to relieve the gloom that pressed in upon him.

The room he had been given was large and furnished with a couple of arm-chairs, a settee, a writing-desk, private phone, private bath and a whole series of lamps that could turn the lighting from garish to downright seductive at the touch of a few switches.

These things Paul noted and, in a somewhat surly way, appreciated. But right now what he appreciated more were the bottles of gin and whisky that he had found, along with a sealed envelope on the writing-desk. A card attached to the Scotch read 'With the compliments of J. J. Huxter.'

A whisky, large, on the rocks, was precisely what Paul needed now. He pushed the bell marked 'Waiter', and almost at once there was a discreet tap on the door.

"Come in," Paul yelled.

Two men, one thin, one plump, came along the brief passage and into the bedroom, where they stood side by side like the figure 10, smiling and bowing. They both wore crisp white coats and neatly pressed black trousers, and the thin one, who was the elder by about fifteen years, said: "*Buenos dias, senor.*"

"Hello," Paul said. "Who are you?"

The thin one said: "I am Josef, senor, and this is Miguel, who is my nephew and my assistant. Alas, he speaks very little English but I am teaching him, senor."

Josef spoke very good English, albeit with a definite American accent. He was slim, rather than thin, graceful as a flamenco dancer. His hair was thick and black, his skin swarthy and shiny and he seemed to have an improbable number of large, white teeth.

"We have been instructed to attend to the guests of Mr. Huxter," he said. "If there is anything you desire ... ?"

Paul raised an eyebrow, a habit, he feared, that he had contracted from Neddy Masters who had doubtless learned it, in turn, from Cary Grant.

"I'd like some ice," he said.

"Ice. Of course, senor." Josef turned to Miguel, spoke quietly to him in Spanish and, when his nephew and assistant had gone, said: "That is all, senor?"

"I think so. Except for my hand luggage. Do you think you could find that for me?"

Josef smiled. "It is here already, senor. In the wardrobe opposite your bathroom. I brought it up myself."

"Thanks." Paul took a hundred peseta note from the roll in his pocket and handed it to the man.

Miguel came back with the ice and a bottle opener and placed them, ceremoniously, beside the gin and the whisky. Paul gave him a hundred pesetas, too. I must be mad, he thought. That's twenty-five bob I've given the pair of them for damn all.

Josef and Miguel thanked him, no more and no less profusely than the tip demanded, and left. At the door Miguel stood to one side to allow Josef, his uncle and his superior, to go first. The door closed silently behind them.

Paul filled a long, slender glass with ice and poured whisky over it until the pale gold liquid rose to just under the rim. The room was hot and he felt sticky and uncomfortable. But the whisky helped. It went down, cold and smooth, and when he had finished it his temper was a lot better.

He poured another one.

Neddy Masters had signed them in at the reception desk downstairs and then left them. "I've got work to do at the studios. Why don't you all have a little rest and then we can meet in the bar. About sevenish. Let's do a little free-loading tonight, get a little drunk, see the night life ..."

Paul, Emma and Grainger had come up to the second floor together in silence. Between Paul and Grainger an instant dislike had shown itself at the airport and Emma, realising this, had tried just once to inject a little brightness into the atmosphere. But whatever it was she had planned to say died stillborn on her lips for lack of a sympathetic audience. The two men spent the short interval in the lift scowling at their shoes.

Their three rooms, they discovered, were next door to each other, Emma's being in the middle.

"See you in the bar then," said Emma.

"Sure," said Grainger.

Paul merely grunted and the three doors closed simultaneously.

About sevenish. Well, there was plenty of time. He finished his second highball, undressed and took a cold shower. Then he had a third drink.

Most of the symptoms of malaise and ill-temper had vanished by the time the glass was empty and he felt light and cheerful. He hung his slacks, with the automatic still inside them, in the wardrobe and put on a fresh suit.

When he had dressed he put his wallet, cigarettes and lighter in his pockets and noticed again the envelope that lay beside the bottles. His name and his room number were typed upon it.

He opened it. Inside were about £20 worth of pesetas and another little slip that said: 'With the compliments of J. J. Huxter.'

Paul shrugged, put the money back in the envelope, the envelope back on the desk and looked at his watch. He had now been at the hotel for nearly an hour and a half and there was still no sign of Blake.

He picked up the phone and asked the operator if any messages had come in for him. None had.

Very well. More than two hours remained to be filled before the rendezvous in the bar and he had nothing much to do. If Blake wouldn't come to him, he would go to Blake.

He checked his appearance in the wall mirror by the door and went out—just in time to see Emma and Grainger disappearing into the lift at the far end of the corridor.

They looked, he was displeased to note, rather happy. By the time Paul reached the vestibule they had vanished. Where he wondered, suspicion welling up again—sightseeing? Or to keep a rendezvous?

Either way there was little he could do about it at the moment. He went outside and found a cab.

The address he wanted, Blake's address, was just off the Avenue Jose Antonio in the city's main shopping area. Walking distance, really, from the Peniscola but in the dusty heat of the afternoon he decided to take a taxi anyway.

He lay back in his seat and looked with only perfunctory interest at the landmarks he passed on the short journey, the sixty-foot high statue of Columbus, the post office that looked more like a royal palace than most royal palaces, the naval ministry next door. He got out at the Continental Hotel and paid off the cab driver, then walked back down the Gran Via until he found the street he wanted.

Paul knew little enough about the habits of the secret service but one thing he had learned from the movies and paper back thrillers was that agents never approached their objectives directly. They always paid off their taxis a few blocks away and covered the rest of the distance on foot to make sure nobody was following them.

Nobody was following Paul.

Blake's street was narrow and shady, the air cooler there than it had been in the wide, sunlit avenue he had just left. Blake's place was a men's boutique, rather chi-chi, with a nice line in black suede jackets discreetly modelled in the windows.

Few people were about. A very old woman in black was shuffling away at the far end of the street. A little boy was sitting on the kerb outside a shoe shop, and a man in a blue jacket was lounging at the solitary table outside the café opposite the boutique.

Paul went into the shop and made a casual examination of some ties on a rack beside the counter. After a moment, a door at the back opened and a dapper young man approached him.

"Good afternoon, senor," he said in Spanish.

"Good afternoon. Could I see Mr. Blake, please?"

The young man looked as regretful as only the Latin races can. It obviously grieved him deeply to have to break the sad news. "I am sorry, senor. Mr. Blake is not here."

Paul held a tie against his coat and surveyed the effect in the mirror. "Any idea when he'll be in?"

"Tomorrow, I hope, senor. He is not in Madrid at the moment."

Paul frowned. Was this good or bad? He gave the question brief thought then dropped it, since, not knowing the circumstances of Blake's absence, he was unlikely to arrive at any accurate conclusion. "Where is he?"

"I do not know, senor."

"Pity." Paul tried another tie and liked it better. "How much is this?"

"Three hundred and fifty pesetas, senor."

"How much?" Paul dropped it as if it was hot. That was about two pounds. More. "Bit steep, isn't it?"

"It is imported, senor, from one of the most exclusive fashion houses in Italy." Contempt floated like an iceberg in the young man's voice, nine-tenths of it concealed by a veneer of politeness.

"I think I'll leave it," Paul said. "Perhaps some other time ..."

"But of course."

Outside, across the street, the man in the blue coat was still sitting at his table. He wore huge round sunglasses and a ghastly green straw hat pulled down low over his forehead. He seemed to be asleep. All right for some people, Paul thought.

He walked back to the Avenue Jose Antonio and found another cab. Ten minutes later he was back at the hotel and knocking on Emma's door. There was no reply. She must still be out with the bastard Grainger. He knocked on the bastard Grainger's door. No reply there, either.

Oh, well, he thought, and went to lie down on his bed while he reviewed the situation.

Damn Blake for being away. Without his instructions Paul had no idea what to do. What did people do in his position?

He could, he supposed, have followed Emma and Grainger when they went out, for it was by no means impossible that they were working together as contacts between Mandrake and the Russians. But, on the other hand, why follow them? Why not follow Neddy Masters? Or, taking it a further step forward, why restrict himself to any of these? If the person he was looking for was connected with the Pontius Pilate film, it could well be that Paul had not met him—or her—yet.

So tailing people around all day was not the answer, even if he had any idea how to go about it, which he hadn't. In any case it would need about a dozen men to do it properly.

What, then, was the answer? There must be something he could do. Anything would be preferable to sitting, or, in the present instance, lying around doing nothing at all.

Well, he thought, he could at least do the routine things. Like keeping his eyes open, his ear to the ground, his shoulder to the wheel, his ... oh, balls, he said, and abandoned that line for the present.

He would just watch out, that was all. And, if the opportunity presented itself, he would take a look round the rooms of the journalists and film people staying at the hotel. Blake might not approve but since Blake wasn't around to say so, Paul would simply have to use his own initiative.

For want of anything better to do and out of a nagging conviction that he ought to be doing something more constructive than lying on his bed, he was about to get up and start searching Emma's room right away, for no other reason than that hers was the nearest, when he heard her come back.

That meant Grainger would be back with her. And Masters was very likely in his room, too.

Some other time, Paul thought, wearily. Anyway, he was by no means sure how to get into the others' rooms. He had no skeleton keys and he could hardly stand out there in the corridor cheerfully picking the locks.

Better to wait. By tomorrow Blake should be back. Then perhaps, they could really get started.

CHAPTER EIGHT

A NIGHT WITH THE BOYS

T WAS about 7.15 when Paul went down to the bar. He had showered again and shaved and, though he felt a little tired, the alcohol he had drunk during the day was still giving him a lift. Besides which, he had decided on a plan for the night.

Free-load, Neddy Masters had said. Get a little drunk. See the night life. Right then. That was the part he would play. He would drink a good deal, appear to get drunk and watch and listen. He might not learn much but at least such conduct would have the effect of making Paul himself seem harmless, which would not do his cover any damage.

Emma and Grainger were sitting over in the corner with a small, bald fat man in glasses. They did not notice Paul come in. Or if they did, they pretended not to.

Hell with you, he thought and turned to the bar. Neddy Masters was standing there, ordering cigarettes.

"Ah. Paul. Come and join us."

Paul climbed on to the bar-stool beside him. "Let's have one here first. What'll it be?"

"My dear Paul," said Masters. "Huxter-Magnus is paying for all this. Keep your money in your pocket." He called up two whiskies.

Then he said: "Did you find an envelope in your room?"

"With twenty quid in it? Yes. What's it for?"

Masters surveyed him over the edge of his glass. The cool, amused Cary Grant look. "You've heard of front money, I suppose?"

"Vaguely. That's the money put up at the start when you're making a film, isn't it?"

"Something like that. Well, Mr. Huxter calls your twenty quid tail money. Get it? I mean, he's a man of the world, you see. He believes that man cannot live by bread alone, that he needs what Mr. Huxter is pleased to call a bit of tail occasionally."

"You mean he's prepared to give me, a complete stranger, twenty quid to go and get laid?"

"If that's what you want to do with the money, yes. Officially, it's for out of pocket expenses. When Mr. Huxter entertains a visiting journalist he likes to do the job properly."

"Very nice of him," Paul said dryly. "Of course, looked at another way, it might be described as a bribe, don't you think?"

Masters pursed his lips and stared thoughtfully at the array of bottles at the back of the bar. "Well, insurance, perhaps."

"Meaning that if I take the money I'm not likely to knock him in anything I write? Bit optimistic of him. I may have my price but I like to think it's higher than twenty quid. Anyway, what happens if I *do* knock him? Does he ask for his money back?"

"He never has yet. Of course, it's always possible. He's a somewhat unpredictable man."

Paul finished his drink, wincing as the last lump of ice brushed painfully against a sensitive tooth. "On the whole, I think I'll leave that money where it is."

Masters looked at him solemnly. Then he grinned. "I think you're being a bit over-cautious but you're probably right. One more drink?"

"Thanks."

They sipped their second drinks more slowly. Paul asked: "Who's the fat chap at the table?"

"You've not met him? That's Big Bill Breugelhoffer."

"Broogle—what?"

"Hoffer. He's the American publicist on this great artistic epic of ours. It's an Anglo-American production, you see, so we have to have an Anglo-American publicity set-up. You'll like Big Bill. Nice little bloke. Drink up and I'll introduce you to him." Paul drank up and was introduced.

You'll like Big Bill, Masters had said, and quite clearly Big Bill intended to be liked. On introduction he seized Paul's hand and clung to it with every evidence of joy, pumping it up and down with an effusive two-handed grip, as if it was too precious to let go. "Paul, it's great to meet you. Neddy has told me so much about you. It's good to have you aboard on this trip and I mean that. Sincerely."

Paul made the right responses but was rather more restrained about it and studied Breugelhoffer with care. The man was about five feet two in height and four feet six in girth. He looked, if the thing were possible, like an All-American Pickwick and, if not exactly the likeliest of Paul's suspects, he was without doubt the roundest.

"Sit down, sit down," he said, making room on the bench seat for Paul to sit beside him. A waiter crept up, removed the empty glasses and came back immediately with full ones, including a very large Scotch on the rocks for Paul.

"Well, this is great," Breugelhoffer said. "Real great. The whole gang together at last. What do you say we celebrate? Let's all go out and set this old town on fire. What do you say?"

Masters smiled and nodded. Emma said "Fine." Grainger said it was okay by him. Paul said nothing.

He had just noticed that Grainger's hand was resting lightly, quite casually, almost absent-mindedly, on Emma's knee. Jealousy stabbed him in the heart. For a moment he had an urge to hurl himself across the table and grab Grainger by the throat.

Then the moment went on its way and he heard Breugelhoffer say: "Well, what do you say, Paul? What do you say, feller?"

He took a swig of his drink. Even the whisky was bitter in his mouth. "What I say," he said, "is that as far as I'm concerned you can bum the bloody place down."

Celebrate? What had he got to celebrate?

Several drinks later they were seated round a table in a restaurant that had once been the home of a Spanish grandee. Dark oak panelling on the walls, thick red carpets on the floors, discreet lighting in the corners, candles and silver cutlery on the tables. Gloom and depression in Paul's heart.

Grainger had his arm around the back of Emma's chair and every now and then his fingers brushed softly against her arm. He talked exclusively, endlessly to her, in whispers most of the time so that Paul had been unable to exchange more than a few words with her.

Instead he communed with a glass of wine, or rather several glasses of wine. Yet he was not drunk. Frequently, when his companions' attention was partially engaged elsewhere, he made a great business of grabbing the bottle and filling his glass. But since the glass was never more than a quarter empty in the first place he gave the overall impression of having had considerably more to drink than he had in fact drunk.

Still, he was uncommunicative and remote and apparently preoccupied with establishing some kind of Spanish AllComers' record for wine consumption and had, long ago, opted out of the conversation.

This state of affairs had existed through the first three courses of dinner, was existing still at the coffee stage and looked like going on for ever.

It might well have done so had not the arrival in the room of a man and a woman drawn Breugelhoffer and Masters smartly to their feet in attitudes of attention.

"J.J.!" yelped Breugelhoffer, as if welcoming the Second Coming, and, taking the man by the arm, presented him to the company. "Paul, Emma, Larry I want you to meet Mr. Huxter. Mr. Huxter this is …"

"I know," said Huxter. He shook hands with them all, murmuring their names as he did so. "Miss Dane, Mr. Baker, Mr. Grainger."

He was not very much taller than Breugelhoffer and only slightly more slender. His hair was white and thick, cut close to the scalp and he wore an air of calculating *bonhomie*. Paul wondered whether the meeting and the trick of remembering all their names had been rehearsed. "Glad to meet you people," Huxter said. "Sorry I wasn't around to welcome you in at the hotel but I was all tied up at the Studios."

He turned to the woman who had come in with him—a tall sensational blonde in a black dress so tight that it seemed to prohibit any movement more strenuous than breathing.

Paul sat back in his chair and stared at her. She was worth staring at. Her eyes were blue and bold, her mouth red and ripe and her breasts pointed arrogantly towards the far corner of the ceiling. They were large and round and firm, like twin Dunlopillo cushions offering rest and solace to the weary.

Paul suddenly felt very weary and much in need of rest and solace.

"Miss Dane, gentlemen," said Huxter, "may I present my lady wife?"

The Lady Wife's gaze went from one to the other, almost ignoring Emma but lingering for a moment on Paul and again on Grainger. "Pleased to meet you," she said. Her voice was a little flat but, Paul reflected as he made signs to the waiter to bring him another drink, who was perfect?

Even Grainger seemed to have succumbed to those obvious charms, for he had taken his arm away from Emma's chair and was sending silent messages of lust across to the Lady Wife with his eyes.

"Well," said Huxter, "I'm glad we all made contact and I'm only sorry I can't stay and talk to you now. But there's a guy waiting to see us back at the hotel. Work all day, work all night. That's show business."

"Sure is, J.J.," said Breugelhoffer. "You know, you really ought to ease up a little."

"That's what the Lady Wife keeps telling me. Ain't that right, honey?"

The Lady Wife nodded briefly. Her thoughtful gaze was still alternating from Paul to Grainger. She did not look as if she would care all that much if her husband dropped down dead there and then from overwork.

"But don't worry about me, Bill," Huxter said. "The Lady Wife takes good care of me. Ain't that right, honey?"

This time she ignored him entirely. She was looking at Paul and the tip of her pink tongue was running slowly across her lower lip. Paul watched its progress, fascinated. The way she was doing it, the simple action of moistening her lips was one of the most erotic things he had ever seen.

Huxter said: "Well, see you on the set tomorrow. We'll all have a good talk then. I got a lot to tell you. But for now ... duty calls. Come on, honey."

Quickly, as the Huxters turned away, Emma got up and said: "Could you give me a lift back to the hotel?"

Equally quickly Grainger transferred his lust from the unattainable Lady Wife to the apparently unattached Emma. "I'll take you," he said.

"No, no," she said. "You stay with the others and help them set the town on fire. I'd like an early night and, besides, I feel sort of outnumbered here."

Huxter chuckled. "That's it, honey. Let the boys get on with their fun. I figure a girl might be a little *de trop* where they're heading. Oh, incidentally, did you fellers get your tail money all right?"

"Thank you, yes," Grainger said, as he sat down again. Paul felt a momentary bond of kinship with him as he realised that Grainger's reaction to the tail money must have been as bleak as his own.

"What's tail money?" Emma asked. Huxter laughed, and Masters and Breugelhoffer had a race to see who could join him laughing first. Breugelhoffer won by a short guffaw.

When the laughter had stopped—Huxter stopped first, Breugelhoffer almost made it a dead heat and Masters, beaten again, cut a final Ho-ho in half as he came in third—Huxter said, "Well, have fun you guys," winked and left them, shepherding Emma and the Lady Wife towards the door. The two women made a fascinating contrast, Emma lithe and dark, the Lady Wife blonde and voluptuous. But now that the initial impact had passed and he could no longer see that pink tongue snaking its way around her lips, Paul knew which of the two he would rather have.

Not that he was ever likely to get the chance, he thought, gloomily. Emma had ignored him all night. He had ruined his chances there, all right.

"Where's that bloody waiter?" he said.

The waiter came and went and Grainger said: "Well, well, well. I'd hardly have recognised her."

"Who?" said Masters.

"Whatsername, the Lady Wife. You know who she is, don't you? You know, Paul, surely?"

"No idea. Never seen her in my life." He made his voice slurred, the words running into each other, blending together incoherently. He reached for his drink.

"Tell us about her, Larry," said Breugelhoffer, his eyes glinting behind the thick glasses as the sweet smell of scandal wafted to his sensitive nostrils.

Grainger took his time about lighting a cigarette, enjoying the attention they were giving him. "Well," he said, at length, "she used to be London's best known professional corespondent."

"You're kidding!" Breugelhoffer and Masters leaned forward, the former flushed and excited, the latter looking like Cary Grant in one of his more serious roles. Even Paul, apparently tipsy though he was, listened with care. Huxter and the Lady Wife had gone into his mental notebook as Suspects five and six and anything he could learn about either might be important.

"She was never mentioned by name in the Divorce Courts, of course," said Grainger. "She was always Miss X. Got away with it for, oh, three or four years. She must have been in about a dozen divorce cases in that time and always cases with well known people involved."

"Howja … how do you know that?" asked Paul, belching politely.

"Used to see a lot of her when I was on the gossip column, I never actually spoke to her but she was at all the big parties, usually with some rich bloke in tow. Everyone knew about her."

Breugelhoffer licked his lips. "She made a living out of this co-respondent business?"

"Are you joking? She made a fortune. She became a sort of vogue. No smart man really felt himself properly divorced unless she was the Miss X in the case."

Grainger paused. "I'm trying to think what her name was."

"Anne something," said Masters.

"Huggins. That's it, Anne Huggins. She changed it to Anne Hathaway when she became an actress. That was when she was mixed up in that film producer's divorce. Bertie Slater, remember? He put her in a couple of his films and she gave up the co-respondent game after that. Then Huxter met her and married her within a month."

"I wonder if he knows," said Breugelhoffer, wiping his glasses on the table-cloth. "I bet he doesn't. Oh, boy, imagine his face if you told him." His round body shook with mirth. "She's a gorgeous piece of ass, that's for sure."

Grainger nodded. "Rattles away like a belt-fed mortar, they tell me."

Breugelhoffer came back from the erotic dreamland to which Grainger's story had sent him and sighed. "Oh boy. I just keep on wondering what J.J. would say if he only knew. Why did she give the game up, though, if she was making so much dough at it?"

Grainger shrugged. "Ambition, I suppose. She probably wanted something more respectable."

"Well, I know what I want," said Breugelhoffer. "I want a damn good lay, that's what I want. You just put me right in the mood for it, Larry."

And so they went off to get Breugelhoffer a lay, and for Paul the night became a series of barely connected nightmare incidents.

For suddenly he was drunk. Really drunk. Stoned-out-of-his-mind drunk and afterwards he could never remember exactly at which stage he got like that.

He remembered leaving the restaurant and getting into a taxi and going to a bar and someone saying: "Come on, let's have a special. Pedro, mix us a special," and after that it was all like something seen dimly in a November fog.

Just now and then he would have moments of clarity as if the night were a kaleidoscope that stopped from time to time so that for a while the patterns became clear …

They were in this brothel, or at least it seemed to be a brothel. Somebody had said it was a brothel. Who had said it was a brothel? He couldn't remember but somebody had.

There was this band and a rather bad blues singer and lots of waiters rushing about between lots of tables and there were women everywhere, necking and dancing with flushed, heavy-breathing men.

There was all this cigarette smoke, blue-grey and hanging in a cloud just below the ceiling. And the noise of the band. And the singer who kept hitting sour notes. And the waiter who kept filling his glass. And …

"Where are we? Wassa time?"

"Hello. He's with us again."

" 'Nother drink. Wan' 'nother drink."

"Waiter!"

And then they were somewhere else and, from nowhere, Huxter and the Lady Wife were at their table and he pointed to them with a whoop, shouting, "Good ol' Huxter. Huxter the huckster."

And somebody said: "Boy, has he got a load on!" And Huxter and his Lady Wife went away and Paul thought of a joke and hurled it at them across the room … "Who was that Lady I saw you with? That was no lady that was my Lady Wife."

And he laughed so much that he fell over backwards and knocked a tray of drinks from a waiter's hands.

And somebody said: "Have another special." And he had another and another and another ...

And then it was another time and another place or maybe it was the same place, and somebody was saying: "Boy, when he ties one on he ties it on with reef knots."

And he was dreadfully unhappy and he began to cry because Emma didn't like him any more and he couldn't bear it. And he thought about the Lady Wife with her incredible breasts and her wiggling behind and he wanted a woman.

"I wan' a woman."

"What's he say?"

"He wants a woman."

"Oh, Christ!"

"Well, he's in the right place for it."

"I wan' a woman. *Now!*"

"For God's sake get him a woman somebody."

And then there was this woman beside him, a blonde woman who was running her fingers along the inside of his thigh and trying to put her tongue in his ear and he said: "Leave us, ev'ybody. I wanna be alone with this woman, this beau'ful woman."

"What's the matter with him now?"

"He says he wants to be alone with her. He wants us all to go."

"For Chrissakes, tell him he can't do it here. He'll have us all arrested."

"All right, I'll tell him ... Listen, you can't do it here, you know ... It's no good, he doesn't know where he is."

"Look, for God's sake, tell her to take him upstairs. Everybody's watching."

"All right, but she wants the money first."

"Well, give it her."

"How much?"

"Nine quid. Sixteen hundred pesetas."

"Nine quid. That's a lot of money for a …"

"Oh, for God's sake, I'll give it to her then. But get him away from here."

"Shouldn't we take him back to the hotel?"

"No, he'll be all right. Give her the money."

And then they were going upstairs and the sound of the band and the bad blues singer receded in the background and they went through a door into a little bedroom and there was just the smell of cheap perfume and this woman taking his clothes off and all he wanted to do was sleep …

CHAPTER NINE

MORNING AFTER ...

H E WAS lying on the floor and the thick pile of the carpet was itchy against his cheek and dusty in his mouth. Not that this made too much difference, because the taste in his mouth was, in any case, foul beyond description.

Like the bottom of a bird-cage, only worse. Like the sole of a fireman's boot. Like a navvy's armpit. Like a belly-dancer's groin.

He tried to get up and collapsed, moaning, as a dozen bolts of lightning struck simultaneously deep within his head.

"Oh, my God, my God ..."

His eyeballs were on fire and his teeth tasted rotten, old and yellow and hideously decayed. The top layer of his tongue seemed to have been burned away by alcohol and cigarette smoke and what was left was raw and filthy.

"I'm ill," he murmured. "I'm very ill."

He crawled towards the bed, grabbed at the coverlet and hauled himself up. A little light—not, thank God, too much—was filtering through the Venetian blinds and when he had grown accustomed to it he realised to his considerable surprise, that he was in his room back at the Peniscola Hotel.

He sat down on the bed, his throbbing head supported tenderly between hands that shook like autumn leaves, and tried to remember how he had got there. He couldn't.

He remembered the girl trying to undress him and that was all. How had he got back here? Who had brought him? The effort of remembering was unbearable. Even thinking comparatively simple things, like 'Who am I?', set that electric storm raging with mindless passion between his temples until it seemed that his entire head would burst.

He wished it would.

"Oh, my God," he said again, softly, because any noise louder than a whisper would have gone through him like a sword.

His watch was still on his wrist and, by holding it close to his face and squinting, he could just make out the time. Ten past five. A.m. or p.m.?

He staggered to the window and peered out through the blinds. A.m. The street outside was still deserted and the air, when he pushed the window open, was cool and fresh.

He took a deep breath of it—and then his stomach treacherously and without warning declared war upon him. Crouching, he shuffled to the bathroom, unfastening his trousers as he went.

The next three hours were spent trekking back and forth between the bathroom and the bed, brief moments of uneasy sleep alternating with long spells of violent activity until he was utterly exhausted.

At one stage he collapsed on the bed, heavy with self-pity. This kind of thing never happened to that secret agent in all those books, old double-o whatsisname. You never heard of him being stuck in a lavatory with his bowels in an uproar. Much pleasanter things happened to him, like being strapped naked to a bottomless chair, having his goolies whacked with a carpet beater.

"I'd change places any time, mate," Paul thought, as he got off the bed again.

From time to time, short piercing memories of the night before came stealing back, bringing with them an overwhelming sense of alcoholic remorse, so that by six-thirty he was almost on the point of phoning Masters and Breugelhoffer and the Huxters, and anyone else who would listen, to apologise and beg their forgiveness for his transgressions.

By eight o'clock he was sleeping again, thoroughly purged inside and as weak as a child convalescing from a serious illness, and it was gone nine before stealthy movements in the room awakened him.

Josef was there with a breakfast tray—coffee, toast, butter and a small glass full of a thick brown liquid, eyeing him with the gravity and concern of a doctor examining a patient.

"Drink this, senor. It will make you better." Josef held out the glass towards him.

"What is it?"

"Medicine, senor. Very effective with ailments such as yours."

"The only ailment I have is the creeping death," said Paul but he drank it, nevertheless, shuddering at its sharp, fiery taste and fell back among the rumpled pillows. "I've not long for this world," he murmured, faintly. "I'm going now."

"Si, senor. But first, perhaps, a little coffee ..." Josef poured the coffee and handed it across, holding on until he was sure that Paul's two trembling hands had the cup securely in their grasp.

Three deep gulps later, Paul said: "Josef, you've dragged me back from the very doorstep of death."

"I used to be a barman, senor. Barmen understand these matters."

Paul drank some more coffee. "I suppose you've no idea how I got back here?"

"By taxi, senor, so I am told by the desk clerk. It was about four o'clock."

A taxi? Who could have put him in that? The girl, probably, though he had no recollection of it.

Josef said: "Shall I take your suit to be pressed?"

"Please."

Josef gathered up the clothes and went quietly away, leaving Paul to his thoughts.

First he thought about people, about Masters, Huxter, Grainger and Breugelhoffer, trying to envisage all or any of them as a spy. He couldn't quite do it.

And he thought about Emma and he couldn't see her as a spy, either, though he knew little enough about her. He knew, because she had told him so on the plane, that she was twenty-five, the daughter of a retired brigadier who bred chinchillas in Warwickshire, rather unsuccessfully, that she had been in journalism for three years and before that had worked for an English firm in Lausanne. He also knew that she had been engaged once but that it never took.

And that was all he did know, apart from really important details, like the fact that she was probably the most attractive girl he had ever met.

When he had wrenched his mind away from Emma, he thought about last night. As a first exercise in undercover work it had been a disaster. All he had got from it was a hangover and a feeling of surprise, almost disbelief, that he had managed to get so drunk. It worried him that this could have happened for it seemed, as far as he could recall, that at one moment he had been sober, and at the next, plastered.

As he analysed his memories of the evening further, the disbelief grew. It just couldn't have happened like that, unless … What? Someone had drugged him? He grinned wryly. "I didn't have much really but some swine must have laced my drinks." How many times had he heard *that* one?

Still …

Question: assuming the drinks were laced, who would have done it?

Answer: the mysterious go-between, perhaps.

Question: why?

Answer: ah, well, yes indeed. Why? As a theory it leaked all over the place and yet, stubbornly, his mind refused to accept that he could have got into that condition wholly unaided.

He pulled the sheet up under his chin and drifted off to sleep, still worrying about it and distressed by a conviction that he was making the most fearful mess of the job he had come here to do.

Half an hour later Neddy Masters woke him up.

"Sorry, old chap," he murmured. Freshly-shaven, neatly pressed, giving off a subtle aroma of Old Spice, he was very Cary Grant indeed this morning. "How are you feeling?"

"Terrible," Paul's voice was faint. "I must have eaten something that upset me."

"Quite." Masters grinned. "Christ, you were stoned last night. I've never seen anyone quite so drunk."

"Please," Paul begged. "Not another word. If there's one thing I can't stand it's someone who was sober telling me what I did when I was drunk. All I want to know is when did you all leave me?"

"When you reeled upstairs after that girl, Rosemary. We waited for half an hour then decided you'd be there for the rest of the night, so we came back."

"We?"

"Big Bill, Larry Grainger and myself."

Grainger. Oh, yes, Paul thought, he would have been there, of course. And by now he would have told Emma all about it and what her reaction would be hardly bore contemplating.

"Ned, what can I say? I'm sorry. Really I am. I don't know what came over me."

Masters chuckled. "Think nothing of it. You were very amusing most of the time. Particularly when you started telling everyone within earshot how much you wanted a woman ... Still, I didn't come here to dredge up memories of your dirty night out. What I came to say was that the rest of us are shoving off to the location and I thought you'd probably want to put that little treat off for a day."

"You're so right."

"If I were you, I'd stay in bed until this evening. Then if you feel up to it you can join us for dinner."

Masters went and stood before the mirror to straighten his tie. "By the way, how was she?"

"Eh?"

"Rosemary. Good?"

Paul stared up at the ceiling. "Do you know," he said in a very small voice, "I just can't remember. I'm not at all sure that anything happened. The state I was in, I don't think it can have done."

Masters chuckled again and went out. Exit, laughing, Paul thought, moodily. He got up, opened the window wide and went back to bed. The shakes had left him now but he still felt very bad and his head ached with a dull persistence.

Sleep, he thought. Good old sleep. The great healer.

But it was not to be that kind of morning. For just as he was dozing off, the door to his room opened, there were light footsteps along the little hall and there she was.

J. J. Huxter's Lady Wife.

Wearing a ladylike grey suit with a long pearl necklace and a most unladylike expression. A predatory expression. A liplicking expression. Her blue eyes glittered and her full, red lips were moist and slightly parted.

"Well now, how are you?" she murmured, gliding across to his bedside with the loping stride of a feline beast of prey.

Her cool hand rested gently on his forehead and her little pink tongue flickered around the corners of her mouth. "I've been hearing things about you."

Paul looked up at her with eyes that bulged with apprehension. Lusting after her in a crowded dining-room was one thing. Having her here, hungry and clearly available, was something else again. Something, in a way, quite terrifying.

And yet, she really was a most remarkably good-looking woman. Unaccountably, considering his weakened condition, a little spark of excitement kicked into life within his breast.

"What kind of things?" His mouth had gone dry and salty.

She smiled, little pointed white teeth shining behind the parted lips, and took off her jacket to reveal a plain, sleeveless blouse.

"They say you're something of a wild man. All wine, women and song."

"You know how people exaggerate." He watched her, still with the mixture of trepidation and anticipation, and wondered what she would do next.

What she did was to sit beside him on the edge of the bed and run her hand from his cheek, down his throat and on to his chest. Her fingers began to massage his left nipple.

"You know you're a good-looking boy?"

He moved a little away from her. "Could I," he asked hoarsely, "have a cigarette, please?"

"Of course." She leaned across him, her pearls lashing his face, and reached for the cigarettes on the bedside table.

Still leaning across him she put a cigarette in her mouth, lit it and placed it between his lips and blew a soft cloud of smoke into his face. He coughed, as the smoke crawled, tickling, up his nose and down to his lungs. For one detached moment, he wondered which was stronger in him, fear or excitement.

Almost casually, she pulled the sheet down and away from him and started to unbutton his pyjama coat.

"Hey!" he said and now, there was no doubt about it, apprehension was beating hell out of all his other emotions. "What about your husband?"

"Miles away," she whispered, her lips brushing his, one deft hand doing things to the cord of his pyjama trousers.

"Steady on. Not so fast." He reached down and grabbed her wrist—just in time—and tried to wriggle out from under her but she was lying across his chest and, in his present enfeebled state, he found it almost impossible to move.

"Lie still," she breathed.

And now … Oh, God, where was her other hand? He held one but where was the other? It wasn't doing anything to him so it must be, it had to be, doing something to her …

It was, in fact, unfastening her blouse, which, in a moment, fluttered down to the floor behind her like a white flag of surrender.

At this point the Puritan within Paul made a valiant, if kill-joy, attempt to make its voice heard. But there was nobody listening. The blood zipped round Paul's veins as if his heart had gone berserk and the drumming in his ears drowned out all warning sounds.

He tried to cry "Stop!", or maybe just "Wait!" but the word never got beyond the back of his throat for her mouth pressed hard down upon his, her tongue reaching out greedily towards his tonsils, and all sorts of things happened at once.

With a wiggle and a jiggle and a twist, her fingers moving efficiently about their business, she got rid of her skirt, hurled away her brassière kicked the sheet clear of the bed and rolled in beside him.

Once more Paul's resistance, its back firmly to the wall, made a bid for supremacy, a last desperate effort before it finally dissolved.

"This is crazy," he said, croaking. "I hardly know you ..." But she did not seem to hear him.

With astonishing swiftness she grabbed him, pulled him, winded, down beside her and hurled herself upon him. Somewhere along the line she had lost her pants and now all she wore was the string of pearls and the most devastatingly ravenous expression Paul had ever seen.

He had a final moment of doubt as they clutched each other. "I don't think ... I can't ..." But to his surprise, he found that he could.

She left him lying, dazed, on the bed. As quickly as she had taken them off, she put her clothes back on again, smiled briefly down at him and went to the door.

"Be in my room at eleven tonight," she said, in a business-like way. "Room 212. My husband won't be there." And then she was gone.

A few minutes later Paul heaved himself wearily up in his bed and reached for his pyjamas.

"Raped," he murmured, wonderingly, to himself. "I've been raped."

Later still he had recovered sufficiently to get up and dress himself, though he found that he was even weaker than before, which, in the circumstances, was not altogether surprising.

He put on a dark blue sports shirt and a pair of off-white slacks. Casual, slip-on shoes and heavy sunglasses completed the ensemble. In the mirror he looked gaunt and wan, like a man recovering from something.

He felt better though when he got outside, and the comparatively cool air streaming in through the open windows of the taxi took the recovery a stage further.

Just as he had done the previous day he got out at the Continental Hotel and walked the rest of the way to Blake's boutique. Still nobody followed him.

The same young man was behind the counter in the shop. The instant smile that he wore for greeting customers vanished when he recognised Paul.

"Senor Blake is still away." he said.

"Oh." Paul had not anticipated this. The agent's continued absence, though doubtless easily explained, was nevertheless annoying. Paul was eager to get to work to justify himself. But without Blake he had little idea of where to start.

"Do you know where he is?" he asked.

"This morning he was at Valencia. He telephoned to me from there."

That was better. It was somewhere around Valencia that Mandrake had his villa. Blake must be there, following the former Cabinet Minister's trail from source.

"When will he be back?"

"The day after tomorrow, senor."

Paul sighed. He seemed to be going around in ever-decreasing circles. At this rate the whole affair would be over before he was even given his first briefing.

"Did he leave any message for me?"

"No," the young man said. "He left no message for anybody."

"Well, where can I call him?"

"I've no idea. He has left Valencia and I do not know where he is now."

"Damn. Listen. If Mr. Blake phones again, tell him Mr. Baker is waiting for him at the Peniscola Hotel."

"Yes, senor. I will try to remember."

Paul slammed the door hard as he went out. It must have been the tie, he decided, walking back to the Gran Via. That's why he doesn't like me, because I wouldn't buy that tie. Well, he was damned if he was going to pay more than two pounds for a tie he could get in London for thirty bob and he would tell Blake so when he saw him. If he ever saw him, which was beginning to seem increasingly unlikely.

He found a taxi, returned to the hotel, took his clothes off and went back to bed. He had got the shakes again.

When he woke up it was evening and Emma was sitting on the other bed, smoking a cigarette in a long black holder and watching him. She was wearing a light, off-white dress that looked as if it might have been made by Mary Quant or a similarly cool young designer. Very simple with a kind of sash round the hips. For some reason he thought of the opening lines of a Fleet Street fashion queen's report from the Paris dress shows—"Busts are out this year and everything of importance happens around the hips ..."

"Hi," said Emma.

"Hi." There was something about her that made his heart beat just a little faster whenever he saw her. Perhaps it was the way the black hair swept round to rest against her cheeks. Perhaps it was the grave, yet slightly mocking, expression in her blue eyes. Or perhaps it was the exciting litheness of her slim but very feminine body. Whatever it was, the effect it had on him was shattering.

"How do you feel?" she asked.

He thought about it. On the whole he felt pretty good now that he had rested.

"Lousy," he said.

"I'm sorry." She didn't sound sorry.

"Don't be. I asked for it."

Suddenly she grinned and he started yearning for her all over again. There was a dimple that he had never noticed before in her right cheek.

"You did rather, didn't you?" she said. "Is it true what they told me?"

He looked at her cautiously. "Depends what they told you."

"Oh, you know. That you got terribly drunk and started shouting things at the Lady Wife and insisted on having a woman and ..."

"Stop! I can't bear it." He plunged his head under the sheet and his voice filtered through, muffled and remorseful. "I don't know what I did last night and I don't want to know."

"But," she persisted, "you did go off with a woman, didn't you? A rather old hostess in a night club, Neddy Masters said. Was she a prostitute? And what happened? Do tell me. I've always wanted to know what happens when a man goes with a prostitute—what the procedure is, I mean? Do you pay her before or after? And what do you talk about?"

"I don't know what she was," Paul said. "Honestly, I don't know anything about her."

"Did you sleep with her?"

He emerged from under the sheet. The blue eyes were watching him intently, as if his answer was very important.

"Would you believe me if I told you I didn't remember?"

"I don't know. I might."

Thoughtfully, she put out her cigarette and crossed her legs, revealing a momentary glimpse of sun-bronzed thigh. Paul compared her warm, tanned skin, with the almost decadent whiteness of the Lady Wife and wondered guiltily how he could have succumbed so easily that morning.

"It's true," he said. "Actually, I don't think I can have done. I don't think I was in a condition to sleep with anyone."

She smiled. Softly, she said: "I'm rather glad."

He reached out, impulsively, to take her hand but she moved a little away, leaving him there with one arm dangling foolishly in mid-air. "I must get ready for dinner," she said. "Are you coming down?" He shook his head. "I don't think I could face it, and I don't think I could face the others. Particularly the Huxters."

She stood up, smoothing her dress down around her hips. Everything of importance, he mused, watching her hands, happens around the hips …

Casually, she said: "She's rather lush, isn't she?"

"Who?"

"The Lady Wife. Mrs. Huxter."

"Oh, ah," he said, making it sound as non-committal as he could. "Why do you ask?"

"Just curious. Oh, well, I must be off."

He watched the slight sway of her hips—what was this thing he had all of a sudden about hips?—as she walked to the door. "I might be down later," he said. "Will you be around?"

"Possibly. They tell me there's a nice little night club in the basement. I might go down there after dinner."

"With Grainger, I suppose," he said.

She shrugged. "Or Neddy Masters. Or even Big Bill Breugelhoffer. I have quite a harem, you know."

At the door she turned and winked and went away. Paul lay back in bed.

One way or another it had been quite a day.

CHAPTER TEN

STRANGER IN A ROOM

A SLIGHT breeze had come up with the night and now it brought the smell of the flowers and the lemon trees drifting up to the balcony.

The night was very dark and in the garden there was only the faint, multi-coloured glow of the fairy lights. Away over to the right the street lamps and the car headlights on the Paseo de la Castellana cut up the darkness, making a series of white streamers in the black.

Standing on his balcony, his eyes grown accustomed to the night, Paul looked down into the garden. It was empty, which was just the way he wanted it.

He smoked a cigarette to calm his nerves, shielding the glowing tip with his hand so that nobody looking up would notice him, and gauged the distance between his balcony and the one outside Emma's room.

The plan was simple.

He would search Emma's room first, then Grainger's, getting from one to the other by means of the balconies. He had no idea what he would find, or even what he was looking for, but he had wasted enough time. There was no point in sitting around waiting for Blake to show up when he might do a little investigating on his own account.

He looked at his watch. Nearly eleven. They would all be downstairs now, finishing dinner. There would be time enough, before they came back, for a quick but unhurried look through the two rooms.

He squeezed out the cigarette with his fingers, dropped the butt on the floor, took a deep breath and clambered on to the balcony wall.

The gap between the two rooms was only a few feet but he mistimed his jump and landed badly. There was a loud crack as the torch in his pocket knocked against the wall. He took it out and tried it, but the bulb had broken and he cursed softly to himself. Still, it was not that important. He could do what he had to do without a torch.

He stood on the threshold of Emma's room, peering inside, trying to get his sight adjusted to the darkness within. The room smelt of woman, of powder and scent and hair lacquer, of oils and creams and bath salts. He thought of frilly sheets and silken nightgowns and long, slender suntanned limbs ...

Inside the room nothing stirred, no one moved.

Paul stepped in, walking cautiously for the darkness was intense. Faintly he saw the outline of the bed and beside it the dressing-table. Making no sound on the thick carpet he walked towards them.

And a man's voice, from somewhere near the door, said in Spanish: "Stand very still, senor."

The words hit Paul like instant paralysis. He stood very still. He could hardly have moved if he wanted to.

The voice said: "Keep your hands away from your pockets. I have a gun and I will not hesitate to shoot if you make any sudden movement."

Paul turned slowly towards the sound, his hands out and well away from his pockets. The man was a vague outline against the wall, identifiable mostly by the white blur of his shirt front and the two white blurs of his cuffs where they showed beneath the sleeves of his jacket.

"Who ... who are you?" Paul asked, hoarsely.

"The hotel detective. And who are you?"

Mentally, Paul estimated the distance between them. It was at least twelve feet, which meant that any attempt on his part to rush the man would be foolhardy, if not fatal. Sweat broke out cold on his forehead.

He said: "Look, I can explain all this. I'm a friend of the lady who has this room ..."

The man laughed. A harsh, unamused sound. "But of course. That is why you came in through the window in the dark."

"No, listen ..."

"That's enough." The man took a few steps towards him, and then stopped. And at that moment the worrying little query that had been nagging away in Paul's mind became clear.

If the man was the hotel detective as he claimed, why were they still standing in the dark? Why had he not switched on the lights and marched Paul out at gunpoint to hand him over to the police? A little shiver of fear rippled up Paul's back.

He said: "You're no more the house detective than I am. Who the hell are you?"

The man was silent for a while. "You're too clever, senor," he said. His hand came up slowly, steadily, and Paul could see the faint glint of the gun barrel.

"You're going to kill me?" His tone was incredulous. Bad enough to have been caught like a thief. But to be shot ... "Why?"

"You don't have to know the reasons." The man came another step closer.

"You're mad," Paul said. "They'll hear the shot. Everyone will hear it. They'll get you before you're out of the room."

The man was leaning sideways, reaching for a cushion from the bed, the gun still aimed at Paul's chest. "This will muffle the sound," he said.

And now, because the man was slightly off balance, his head turned away, and because this was likely to be the only chance he would be offered, Paul acted. He took off in a desperate leap, his fingers clawing for the man's gunhand. For an awful, panic-stricken second he thought he had missed. Then his wrist struck against the man's arm, the gun fell to the ground and the two of them were slammed by the momentum of Paul's leap against the wall.

A hand grabbed Paul around the throat and a fist dug viciously into his stomach. Grunting, he doubled up and the man's knee came up under his chin.

He fell—and felt the gun barrel under his hand. But before he could snatch it up the weapon was kicked away. He looked up in time to see the man's foot coming down towards his face. He rolled aside, grabbed the foot and heaved.

With a yell, the man tumbled backwards onto the bed and Paul sprang on top of him.

For a few moments they grappled silently and then, simultaneously, each broke away and dived for the gun. Their heads cracked together as they reached for it. The man swung out and the back of his fist caught Paul in the throat and sent him staggering backwards towards the door.

The gun lay on the floor near the foot of the bed and the man was on his knees beside it.

Paul seized the door handle, twisted it, pulled the door open and darted out into the corridor, just as the man turned towards him, the gun in his hand.

Then the door was shut and Paul was racing down the corridor towards the lift and praying that it would be there. It was and he dashed in as the doors were closing.

His legs were trembling and he was sore in several parts of his body but his overall sensation was one of relief and with it, a sense of excitement.

Whoever he was the man had been no burglar, that was for sure. Even less was he the house detective. And so ...

Paul had made himself believe that his journey would not be in vain but until this moment he had not quite believed it. Now he was sure.

The man in Emma's room could have been, must have been, only one person, the person Paul had come to Madrid to find—the go-between for Mandrake and the Russians ...

A little Latin-American combo was playing soft music at the far end of the room and a dozen couples were doing a sedate tango on the dance floor.

Emma was sitting alone at a table near the bar, a tall, pale drink in front of her. She smiled as Paul came in and, having located her, came straight towards her.

"Sit down," she said, "and tell me your problems."

He sat down and beckoned with urgency to a waiter. "What makes you think I've got problems?"

"Nobody goes around looking like something out of Chekhov without having problems."

He craned back to look at himself in the mirror behind the bar. His hair was ruffled and his tie was somewhere beneath his left ear. In addition his face wore a worried sort of expression. Was that how people in Chekhov looked? He supposed it must be, if she said so. He straightened the tie, brushed his hair down with his hands, swapped the original expression for something brighter, "How's that?"

She nodded. "What happened?"

"I dressed in a hurry."

"I can believe it. You look as if you've just escaped from some woman's bedroom."

And then he remembered. "What's the time?" he asked.

"Twenty past eleven."

"Oh. God …" He had an appointment for eleven o'clock in the Lady Wife's room and the fact that it had never been made, or indeed, encouraged by him, hardly improved matters. She had, presumably, been waiting for him. He had stood her up. And he had a grave suspicion that she was not the kind to take that sort of treatment lightly.

Emma surveyed him with cold blue eyes. "You had a date?" Her voice had come straight from the deep-freeze.

"What? Oh, no. No, indeed. I was supposed to phone London at eleven, that's all. It doesn't matter."

She started to say something but he interrupted her quickly. "Let's dance," he said.

The band was playing a twist and playing it with such determination that conversation, luckily, was out of the question. They stood facing each other, twisting frenziedly.

She did it very well, with an effortless and unconscious sensuality which, anywhere else but on a dance floor, would have got her arrested.

This fact Paul duly noted but somehow he was unable to give it his full and appreciative attention. Even the other, glorious fact, that he was here, alone with her at last, Grainger and the others nowhere in sight, did not cause him as much elation as it should have done.

The circumstances were wrong. There were too many problems on his mind.

Looking back on it all, he realised that, when, prompted entirely by fear, he had run from Emma's room, he had thrown aside a chance to discover the identity of Mandrake's go-between. Now, in the safety of this little night club, he realised that he should have stayed, disarmed the man, forced a confession from him.

That was looking at it one way. The heroic way.

Paul, however, all things considered, preferred to look at it another way. The discretion-is-the-better-part-of-valour way. The man had had a gun, he reminded himself, and would, quite certainly, have had no compunction about using it.

Admittedly, Paul had taken the gun away from him once but that was no guarantee that he could do it again. Therefore, if he had stayed to carry on the struggle, he might now be lying dead upstairs. So, he argued, as he twisted down till his backside was almost resting on the floor, he had shown enormous wisdom in getting the hell out of that room as fast as he could.

That, then, was on the credit side. On the debit side he had been a fool to start his search without being armed himself. Everything had been so quiet and uneventful before tonight, that he had set out on his little journey of exploration with no thought for what he might encounter. He would have dismissed as impossible any suggestion that strange men with guns might turn up in darkened bedrooms. Nothing remotely like it had ever happened in Paul's journalistic career.

However ...

Having got out of there alive what could he have done? If he had gone to his own room to get his automatic, two things might have happened. The man might have escaped before Paul got back to Emma's room. Or he might simply have leaped over the balcony into Paul's room and waited there to pick him off as he came through the door.

The very thought of it made Paul feel cold and he was glad when the music stopped and he could take Emma back to the table for a quick drink.

"Why so pensive?" she asked.

"Not pensive, really. I'm just enjoying this."

"This?" She waved a hand to indicate the room and the band, deliberately misunderstanding him. He shook his head.

"This," he said and took her hand in his. She had small hands, with slender fingers, but there was strength there too.

"Well, well, well," she murmured, softly. "Surely you're not in the mood again. Wasn't last night enough for you?"

He flushed and took his hand away but she reached out and seized his wrist. "Come back. I wasn't complaining, was I?"

The band started up again, soft, dreamy stuff and they went back onto the dance floor, holding each other close. For the first time since he had arrived in Spain, Paul began to enjoy himself.

He felt the pride of possession of a man who knows he is with the loveliest woman in the place and the excitement that comes from the knowledge that a conquest which, at one time, seemed impossible, was on the verge of becoming a total success.

After a while he said: "What happened to the others?"

"I don't know. I lost them. I told them I was going to bed and they went out. Why?"

"I thought you were sort of involved with Grainger."

"I sort of was," she said. "But it was more his idea than mine." Her soft, black hair brushed gently against his cheek as he executed a rather tricky step. "Very good," she murmured. "You're not a bad dancer."

There was a lengthy silence as they went round the floor again. Her fingers stroked the hair on the back of his neck.

"Well?" he said on their third time round.

"What?" she said.

"About Grainger?"

She drew back so that she could look at him. Gravely, she studied his face.

"Are you jealous?"

He snorted, as if the idea was ridiculous. "In a word," he said, "yes."

She went back into his arms, snuggling against his chest, her lips close to his ear, her fingers doing nice things to his back. "Good."

"You know what I think?" he said. "I think you're just a teaser."

She laughed. "That's what all the boys say." Again there was silence.

"For God's sake," he said urgently.

She sighed. "Well, I'll tell you. I got sort of involved with Grainger because I had no real alternative. You seemed to lose interest in me as soon as the plane landed and I didn't see any reason why I should be on my own all the time just because you were sulking. I'm glad you snapped out of it, though. Larry's a terrible bore."

The words struck him sweeter than any chord the band had played all night. "Waiter," he said, as they drifted past the table, "Champagne."

"A celebration?" she asked.

"Yes." He kissed her lightly on the ear and she purred, in that pleasant way girls have.

"Careful," she whispered. "They put you in jail here for snogging in public."

At this moment it no longer seemed to matter that she was still high on his list of suspects. For now at least, he saw her only as a beautiful girl who attracted him as no other girl ever had. And, more than anything else in the world, he wanted to go to bed with her.

Two glasses of champagne later he told her so. She considered the matter reflectively. At length … "Slow down," she said. "I need a lot of notice of that kind of question."

"It wasn't a question. It was a statement of fact."

"Same thing." Frowning, she ran a finger down the back of his hand. "I suppose in a way I *am* a bit of a teaser. Lots of girls are. It's a sort of compromise between being all icy and frigid and giving it away to anyone who asks."

She rested her chin on one hand and looked thoughtfully at him. "Besides, I've got old-fashioned principles. I know that some girls just flop on their backs as if it were simply a matter of course. Like giving a man a goodnight kiss. But it's not like that with me. It's not a matter of honour—I mean, it's a ridiculous sort of place to keep your honour, isn't it? But ... well, when I go to bed with a man it must be for a better reason than that he just happens to fancy me. See?"

"I see," he said. Somehow what she said made him feel better. He was long past the stage of demanding that every girl he fell for must be a virgin but he had never really liked girls who were easy. Girls like that made him feel uncomfortable and oddly inferior, as if they were silently comparing his performance unfavourably with the performances of his predecessors.

"I have to be courted," she said, "and made to feel wanted— and not just physically." Swiftly, she leaned over and kissed him on the corner of the mouth but when he tried to return the favour she drew back, out of range. "So if all you want is a body to slake your lust on, you'd better go back to La Nottee."

"La what?" he asked, startled.

"The place you were at last night. That's what it's called. La Nottee. Remember? Where you went about hollering that you wanted a woman." Her fingernails dug savagely into the back of his hand.

Her rapid change of mood puzzled him for a second. Then he understood.

"You're jealous now," he said, delighted.

She lit a cigarette and gave him the full icy treatment with her glorious blue eyes. "As a matter of fact, I am. I was livid when I heard about it. And *how* I heard about it—from Larry Grainger and Neddy Masters and Bill Breugelhoffer and just about everybody else in Madrid it seemed to me."

"But I explained. Nothing happened."

"As far as you remember."

"Well, yes …"

"It's not good enough, my lad. You keep away from these dens of vice in future, you hear me?"

"Yes, dear," he said, meekly.

"All right then. You can dance with me again, if you like."

"I like."

It was two a.m. when they left the night club and by that time his courtship was well advanced, though not he judged, advanced enough for any liberties to be lightly taken.

Outside her room she paused and turned towards him. "This is as far as you go."

"Can't I just come in for a minute?" He had no real hope that she would say yes but it would be nice to know how far his luck could be pushed. At once he found out—not very far, apparently.

"No," she said firmly. "When I ask you to come in—*if* I ask you to come in—it'll be when I'm good and ready. However, since nobody is about you may kiss me goodnight."

Which he did with considerable skill and enthusiasm, using the opportunity to glance over her shoulder through the open door of her room. Everything was perfectly tidy inside, showing no trace at all of the struggle that had taken place there a few hours earlier.

His own room, however, was rather different …

Clothes and papers were scattered all over, the bed covers were in a heap in the corner, the mattress on each bed had been stripped and turned over. The lining of one of his jackets had been ripped out and a shirt had been torn into half a dozen pieces. There was something rather terrifying about such wanton destruction and it shook Paul badly.

He checked the base of his typewriter and the pouch in his slacks for the guns he had hidden. Neither had been taken. Neither, probably, had been discovered.

Looking at the wreckage, he wondered whether the intruder had, in fact, been searching for anything. For it occurred to him that all this mess might have been made as a warning that if he wanted to play the particular game in which he was involved, he must be prepared for it to get rough.

All right. He was prepared.

When he had cleared up the room, he put his automatic in the shoulder holster beside the bed, shut the windows and locked the door. As he undressed, he reviewed, briefly, the situation as it now stood ...

The enemy at last, had shown his hand; something he would not have done if the negotiations with Mandrake had been completed.

Blake would be back the next day and he would know what Paul should do next.

And finally there was Emma. Emma ...

The name was on his lips as he fell asleep and, the traditional, slightly fatuous, smile of the lover would have been there with it but for the one, tiny doubt her memory aroused.

What had the man been doing in her room in the first place?

CHAPTER ELEVEN

NOW BARABBAS ...

THE ROMAN armies stretched out into the distance under a canopy of blue cigarette smoke. A man with a megaphone was shouting "Okay, you guys. Kill those butts." A centurion with a cigar in his mouth was flirting casually with a blonde girl in jeans and a denim shirt.

Despite the brightness of the mid-morning sun, the arc lights blazed down ferociously just in front of where Paul was standing with Masters and Breugelhoffer.

Behind them in a leather armchair perched on top of a contraption like a Wimbledon umpire's ladder sat J. J. Huxter, overseeing operations with the vigilance of a man to whom every lost minute means the waste of someone else's money, and chewing on a fifty-guinea Dunhill straight grain. From time to time, as it failed to draw satisfactorily, he hammered it against the arm of his chair in a way that would have made a Dunhill salesman snatch it from him and give him his money back.

"Come on, you guys, for Chrissake," he yelled. "This is costing a thousand bucks an hour."

"Nearly ready J.J.," said a sallow young man who had been pointed out to Paul as an assistant director.

"Well, for Chrissake," said Huxter.

There were several reasons why Paul had come out on the location of the film that day. In the first place, all his suspects were here. In the second, there was little else he could do until Blake returned tomorrow. And in the third, he had his cover to maintain and the *Sunday Journal's* twenty-five pounds to earn.

Masters had called him up around nine o'clock.

"Fit, old chap?"

"Fine," Paul said.

"Right. We're shooting in the grounds of an old palace out on the Barcelona road. Take about an hour to get there."

On his way downstairs, Paul had run into the Lady Wife. She was coming out of her room and she had her back to him. He paused, wondering whether to walk on before she saw him but decided finally that at least he owed her an apology for last night.

"Good morning," he said, hesitantly. She stiffened but neither turned round nor spoke.

"Look, I'm … I'm sorry about last night. I got held up and couldn't make it. A business thing."

Then she turned and her face was ugly with hate and a rage that was only just suppressed. "I know where you were." Her voice was flat, barely audible. "You were with that little whore from London."

"Hold on …" Paul came gallantly to Emma's defence but his interruption was brushed aside like the feeble thing it was.

"I waited for you. Two hours. And you stood me up. Nobody does that to me. You'll see. Nobody stands me up." Suddenly she took a quick step forward and spat full in his face. "You'll see," she said again. "You'll see."

It had been an unnerving experience and even now, two hours later, the memory still made Paul feel uncomfortable. To make matters worse, the Lady Wife had appeared on the location a little while ago and he lived in dread that she might make a scene in front of her husband.

But in fact when she did come near Paul she merely nodded coldly towards him and said nothing. She looked magnificent in a pair of tight, pink hipster pants and a white silk shirt but Paul found that he had lost all desire for her. It would not have worried him, indeed he would have been immensely relieved, if he never saw her again in his life.

"Come on, come on," Huxter was hollering from his ladder. "Pull your goddam fingers out, why don't you? This is costing *money* ..."

"I always thought," Paul whispered to Masters, "that it was the director who usually did all the shouting."

Masters grinned faintly. "It usually is. But this is a J. J. Huxter movie and on a J. J. Huxter movie nobody else shouts."

Behind the producer's chair was the old palace that had once belonged to the Spanish royal family, a white L-shaped building of more than a hundred rooms, some of which were being used in the film for interior shots.

Beside the palace stood the front wall of the temple, which the film company had erected. And at the other end of the field was the assembled mass of the Roman army marching on Jerusalem. There were about three hundred of them, a motley crew of Spanish extras who trudged sullenly back and forth in the hot sunshine, neither really knowing what they were doing, nor caring. It was a job, wasn't it?

The star of the picture, a thick-set Italian-American with a built-in scowl, was kneeling on the grass in the woollen underwear which Roman officers apparently wore beneath their uniforms, hacking savagely with a knife at a lump of driftwood and deluding himself into believing that he was some kind of a sculptor.

Last year he had believed he was some kind of a painter and the year before that some kind of a composer. The object of art on which he was now working resembled nothing so much as a piece of whittled driftwood but nevertheless it drew forth appreciative murmurs from the admirers crouched by his side.

The director, a man in a floppy blue hat, who had a great reputation as a maker of 'artistic' pictures and despised himself for succumbing to the lure of Huxter's gold, was regarding the Roman army through a view-finder. It was out of focus and he could see nothing, but the mere act of looking through it set him apart as an infinitely higher technician than the assistants around him.

"All set, J. J.," said the sallow young man.

Paul looked round for Emma. He had seen her only briefly that morning, gorgeous in a blue summer dress that hinted coquettishly at the curves it concealed. She was off now interviewing the female star of the picture and would be heavily engaged, one way or another, throughout the day.

Still, there had been time to arrange a dinner date for the evening and Paul was not entirely sorry to be without her until then. At least on his own he had the opportunity to look around.

The Roman armies, cigarettes out and trampled underfoot, conversing together out of the corners of their mouths, were slowly approaching the cameras, their leader, resplendent in bright new armour, striding out ahead.

From the opposite direction, as if coming from the temple, a lone man—the star himself, now also in armour—walked towards them.

Suddenly the two armoured men broke into a run, arms outstretched, their expressions indicating astonished delight, and met with a fearful clashing of breastplates right in front of the camera.

"Pontius!"

"Caligula! You ole …"

"Caligula!" said Paul, baffled. "How did *he* get into this?"

"You may well ask," said Masters, *sotto voce*.

Breugelhoffer switched his cigar from one corner of his mouth to the other. "This is the scene where Pontius and Caligula meet outside the temple in Jerusalem. It's one of the key scenes of the picture."

His face wore a frown of what Paul could only believe was genuine sincerity. Masters, on the other hand, was staring off into the distance as if he had just noticed something of intense interest about twenty-five miles away.

"You must be joking," Paul said. "They weren't even contemporaries."

"It's kind of poetic licence," Breugelhoffer said. "It could have happened, after all. Christ was crucified in Tiberius' time and Caligula, the next emperor, was alive then. Why shouldn't he and Pilate have been buddies?"

"But ..."

"Look," Masters' voice and expression were equally bland, "perhaps Big Bill should explain the picture to you. Obviously you haven't seen the synopsis."

"No, I haven't. It must be a very interesting document."

Breugelhoffer led him a little to one side and they watched while the two actors and the army repeated the same scene a few more times exactly as they had done it at first.

"What we're trying to do," Breugelhoffer said, "is to give Pilate a new image. What our script says, in effect, is that he couldn't have been all bad."

"You mean he's the *hero*?"

"In a way. See, this is the story of Pontius, his life and his women."

"What women?"

Breugelhoffer spat the stub of his cigar onto the ground. "He must have had women, unless you're suggesting he was some kind of a pervert. We've done research on the guy, tried to dig down to the *real* Pilate. Anyway, the Crucifixion and all is just a small part of this movie. The rest is about Pontius himself."

"Yes," Paul said. "I understand that. But why bring Caligula into it?"

"For the orgy scene," Breugelhoffer said, as if explaining something to a particularly unintelligent child.

Paul stared at him. "What?" he said, tonelessly.

"Look, you can't sell a picture on religion alone. De Mille taught us that. You gotta have sex. You gotta have wine, women, song, drunks grappling with virgins. You've … Hell, didn't you ever read the Roman historians?"

"Some," said Paul. "Tacitus, Suetonius …"

"Sure. Now, you remember the story where Caligula goes to a wedding and all of a sudden he gets a hard on for the bride?"

Paul scratched the back of his neck. "I do remember something like that, only your version seems to be a very free translation from the Latin."

"Yeah. Well, at the end of the reception the groom is kissing the bride and suddenly Caligula, who up to now has been getting drunk and grappling with a few virgins, ups and says 'Leave that woman alone. She's *my* wife.' That's when the orgy starts. It's a great scene."

"Yes," said Paul, slowly. "I can well imagine. But aren't there certain inaccuracies in it? I mean, it happened at Rome, not Jerusalem. And besides, Caligula was emperor at the time, not Tiberius."

Breugelhoffer shook his head and looked exasperated. "Look, when you're making historical movies, you have to compress a little. It's, well like I said, it's poetic licence."

Paul glanced across at Masters, who looked back at him, straight-faced. "Perfectly reasonable, old boy," Masters said. But just for a moment the faint beginning of a smile etched itself in around his lips.

A group of legionaries broke away from the main body of the army and threw themselves down on the ground beside Paul and the publicity men. One of them produced a pack of cards, another a bottle of wine. The smell of garlic hovered around them like an extra, tangible presence. Paul and the others moved away.

Just behind Huxter's ladder, a man in a ragged brown cloak sat apart from everyone else, his head bent over something he was reading. There was a relaxed quality about him, a stillness that was impressive and Paul, jerking a thumb in his direction, said: "Who's that?"

Breugelhoffer smiled in a particularly smug way. "Barabbas," he said. "It's interesting you should ask about him. He's a sort of … surprise item, if you like. In a movie like this you need a … well, a sort of additional mysterious quality and he's it."

"What's mysterious about Barabbas?" Paul asked.

"Just our interpretation of him," Breugelhoffer said. "We've looked at him from a different angle. The way we see him, Barabbas must have been a kind of saintly man with some hidden, holy qualities …"

Paul was not surprised. He would not have been surprised if Christ turned out to be the heavy in this picture.

"I'd like to interview Barabbas," he said.

Breugelhoffer shook his head, decisively. "Out of the question. Nobody is allowed to talk to him or take pictures of him or anything. His role is so important, and so unusual, that it can only be appreciated on the screen. We're keeping him under tight wraps until the picture's finished. Right now I'm not allowed to tell you a single thing about him. He has to remain a mystery man."

"A gimmick," Paul said. "I see."

Huxter, descended now from his ladder while a new scene was set up, materialised beside them. "We don't like that word around here, Paul," he said, reprovingly. "We don't ever use it, do we, Bill?"

"Damn right, J.J."

Huxter gave his pipe a resounding crack against the heel of his shoe and blew through it. It gave off a wheezing, whistling sound and a small piece of soggy tar leapt a foot out of the bowl and landed on Breugelhoffer's suit.

"That's better," Huxter said. "Now maybe I can smoke the goddam thing."

Paul studied him carefully as he went through the process of repacking his pipe. Out here on location where he was the supreme boss, Huxter was different. He was sharp and hard and demanding, a miniature dictator.

When they had met briefly the night before last, Paul had seen him as something of a buffoon, with his round, smooth face and his small, fat body. Now, however, it dawned on him that whatever else Huxter might be, he was not a fool. There was a quick, shrewd look in his eyes and a certainty and confidence about his movements. Paul had the feeling that if the film Huxter was making was a load of rubbish, then Huxter knew it and there was a reason for it. The reason, doubtless, being to make money. Huxter was very good at that.

"No, Paul," Huxter said, "we don't like the word gimmick. This is a devout subject and we're treating it devoutly. That's why I don't want any cheap publicity on the guy who plays Barabbas. It's not that kind of movie."

Before Paul could say anything—and there was little he dared trust himself to say in the face of such hypocrisy—Masters gave a discreet little cough. "If you have a minute, J. J. there are one or two things …"

"Sure." Huxter gave Paul's arm a friendly squeeze. "Excuse us a minute, will you, Paul? Don't go away." He moved off with his publicity men following a respectful pace behind.

Paul turned his attention back to the filming. The extras had their cigarettes going again. The man in the toga had his arm round the girl in jeans, with his hand cupped over her breast. She seemed to enjoy that. The director and the cameraman were talking to Caligula, and Pontius Pilate was whittling away at his driftwood. The actor who played Barabbas was still sitting on his own.

On a sudden whim Paul went over and tapped him on the shoulder. "Excuse me," he said. "I know I musn't speak to you but do you mind if I kiss the hem of your garment?"

Slowly, the dark, tanned face turned towards him. The deep, haunting eyes narrowed. In their foliage of golden-brown beard and moustache, the finely chiselled lips curled in a small sneer.

"Piss off," said Barabbas in the accent of the Old Kent Road and went back to his science fiction comic.

As if from nowhere Breugelhoffer and Masters appeared on either side of Paul, their faces grim. Each took him firmly by an elbow like policemen arresting a rioter.

"You didn't talk to him, did you?" Masters asked Barabbas.

The actor shook his head, glanced contemptuously at Paul and spat on the ground.

"Come on, feller," Breugelhoffer said, sounding as harsh as he suddenly looked.

"Idiot," Masters murmured to Paul. "What did you want to do that for?"

He and Breugelhoffer wheeled Paul round and marched him off at a brisk pace to the umpire's ladder where Huxter had once more taken his seat.

Paul stared up at him, like the accused man in the dock. Breugelhoffer and Masters took up their positions a step behind, like jailers. Huxter gazed down, stern as a High Court judge. Paul wondered uneasily what the maximum sentence was likely to be for the crime he had just committed.

Huxter said: "I didn't like that, Paul. I didn't like that one little bit. I trusted you and you betrayed my trust. Now that's bad."

"Oh, come on," Paul protested. "I'm a newspaperman and that fellow over there is a story. What's all the fuss about?"

"I don't like to remind you of this, Paul," Huxter said. "But you're my guest. Now I feel there are certain obligations a guest owes to his host and to my mind what you just did is as much a betrayal of my faith in you as if you had come into my home and tried to seduce my Lady Wife."

Paul felt the blood leaving his face. Could Huxter possibly know?

It seemed he couldn't. For he went on: "I mean that, Paul. What you just did was a betrayal of hospitality. I hate to say that, believe me. I don't want to enter into a discussion of the ethics of your position here, I just want you to know how I feel, rightly or wrongly. And all I want from you is your word of honour that you will not try to interview that particular actor again. Do I have it?"

Paul nodded, sullenly. He felt humiliated but there was little he could do about it.

Huxter beamed, once more the jovial fat man. "That's great. Now we're friends again." Then, raising his voice, he yelled to the assistant director: "Get those goddamned extras off their lazy asses! Let's get this scene moving."

Paul was dismissed or, rather, conditionally discharged. He slouched away, cross and resentful. All the things he might have said came into his mind and he was tempted to go back and start a real row. But it was too late for that. It always was. He kicked viciously at a pebble and watched it clang against the metal side of one of the caravans which the unit used as offices and dressing-rooms.

On the side of this particular caravan in large, pink letters was the legend: 'Mr. J. J. Huxter.'

It was empty and the door was open and Paul went in. To search it now with so many people about was a risky business but, emboldened by anger and acting entirely on impulse, he thought to hell with the risk. He pushed the door shut and looked around.

The interior was decorated in pale blue and orange—blue walls, orange carpet. There was a desk and a filing cabinet, a couple of easy chairs and a bed. Over the bed, a constant inspiration to anyone lying there, was a huge, coloured photograph of the Lady Wife wearing the prim, white dress of a debutante and the provocative smile of a whore.

Paul made sure nobody was approaching and began to search the desk and the cabinet. He did it swiftly and, to his pleased surprise, rather well, missing little and disturbing nothing. Finding nothing, either.

In the whole place the most sinister document he came across was a memorandum to the production manager instructing him to fire his assistant.

Disappointed, Paul went to the door and looked out.

Across the field, the unit had broken for lunch. The stars and the senior technicians were drifting over to the smart little marquee that served as their dining-room. Emma was there with the actress who played Mary Magdalene and Grainger was behind her, talking to Caligula. Huxter went in with the Lady Wife, Masters, Breugelhoffer and a dozen assorted sycophants. Pontius Pilate followed, still hugging his driftwood.

Nearby a large crowd of small-part actors and lesser technicians headed towards a larger, shabbier marquee and the extras were being catered for by a mobile canteen.

The caste system, so rigorously maintained in the movie business, was safe for another lunchtime.

When everyone had settled, Paul went over to the trailer marked 'Publicity' and also, for the benefit of the Spanish 'Publicidad'. It was about the same size as Huxter's but older and sparsely furnished. Two desks, one bearing a card labelled 'William Q. Breugelhoffer', the other labelled 'Ned Masters'. Two filing cabinets. No beds. Publicists, unlike producers, are not encouraged to rest or have intercourse in the firm's time.

Paul searched it all, including the two wastepaper baskets. He found nothing remarkable. What he did find was a discouragingly long list of people connected with the film who had been brought over from London and who, for this reason, could all be regarded as possible suspects.

Discouraged and perspiring in the midday heat he walked over towards the stars' dining-tent, a little hungry and very thirsty, but before he got there a small, dark man in workman's overalls sidled up and pressed a piece of paper into his hand.

"From the lady, senor," he whispered and sidled away again, wearing the pleased smile of a man who has done his bit for Cupid.

The message on the paper read: "Darling, can you meet me in the props department? Now. Very urgent. Love, Emma."

Paul said: "The props department. Where is it?"

The man gestured towards the temple. "Behind there, senor."

Paul gave him twenty pesetas and watched until he was out of sight. Then he hurried over to the temple.

His first reaction to the note had been pleasure at the words "darling" and "love." But now he felt puzzled. What on earth was it all about? Why all the secrecy? And what could be so very urgent, for heaven's sake?

He pushed open the huge, balsa wood door and stepped into, and at the same time, out of the film company's temple, which was simply one plaster-board wall held up by a series of wooden struts. The property department was about a hundred yards behind it. housed in a large, dark and vaguely forbidding old barn.

No sign of life showed from within. Everything was still and even the noise from the dining tents had receded into the distance, like the sound of traffic heard from afar.

Suddenly Paul felt cold. He had an unaccountable presentiment of danger and, as if by instinct, he took his automatic out of its shoulder holster. It had a comforting feel in his hand.

The door to the barn was slightly ajar and he pushed it wide open with his foot, peering into the gloom within. "Emma?" he called, softly. Nothing happened. Nothing moved.

Cautiously, he took a step inside …

There was a blur of movement beside him, something heavy descended with vicious force on his wrist, knocking the gun from his hand. Another blow, on the chest, sent him reeling against the wall. The door slammed shut.

And he looked up to see Barabbas coming at him with a spear in his hand.

CHAPTER TWELVE

... WAS A TEARAWAY

PAUL JUST had time to duck before the point of the spear buried itself in the woodwork, exactly where his head had been a moment before.

"Come on, you bastard," said Barabbas. "Let's 'ave yer." He wrenched the spear from the wall and turned for another attack.

Paul backed away, seeking round desperately for a weapon with which to defend himself.

The man lunged again, the spear passed under Paul's arm and the impetus thrust the two men together. Paul shoved him away and backed off.

"Funny man, aren't yer? With your little jokes about kissing the hem of me garment. Very funny. I'll make yer laugh, though …"

The man reeked of brandy. His eyes were mad, bloodshot. Saliva trickled from the corner of his mouth into his beard and there were great sweat stains on his rough brown tunic.

Paul was sweating, too, but not with the heat. He had a desperate desire to scream for help and it was an effort to fight down and try to control the panic that grew inside him. His breathing was quick and shallow with a trembling sound.

"Scared, eh? You should be. Because I'm going to tear you to bits, you bastard."

They circled warily round each other, the man making swift short jabs with the spear. He was tall, over six foot, and built like a cruiser-weight boxer. But his reactions, slowed by the brandy, were a handicap in this weird manhunt and his balance was slightly wrong.

It was this that gave Paul his chance, for as the man jabbed again he reached a fraction too far and stumbled.

Paul, his own reactions sharpened by fear, leapt upon him, grabbed his arm and pulled him down to his knees. "You bastard," the man said again. He had a very limited vocabulary.

Paul kicked him hard in the chest, lost his own balance and, though he recovered fast, the man was on his feet and charging towards him, the spear outstretched.

Again Paul grabbed it, twisting it upwards and again they were thrown together, their faces so close that Paul could feel the other man's beard rasping against his cheek, could smell the stale breath, could taste the other's sweat in his mouth.

At such close quarters, physical strength was all that counted and Barabbas was the stronger of the two. Slowly, panting, he shoved Paul back and back, forcing the spear down and across Paul's throat.

Paul felt himself weakening, felt the increasing pressure of the haft against his Adam's apple. His head bent forward—and his bulging eyes stared down at the other man's thin sandals.

Frantically, despairingly he brought his heel down hard on the actor's foot, heard the quick, sharp cry of pain and brought it down again and again until something cracked and the pressure on his throat suddenly relaxed.

With a heave he pushed the man away and then, with all the strength he had left, kicked him in the crotch. The man dropped to the floor, doubled up, his hands clutching his groin, his head resting on the ground. An unpleasant animal sound of pain came from his lips.

Paul leaned against the wall and rubbed the sweat off his face. Every limb in his body was trembling. It was an effort to bend down and pick up the fallen spear. His neck was sore and the breath felt hot in his lungs.

Barabbas had collapsed onto his side in a foetal position, moaning. His face was grey with pain and saliva had frothed on his lips and beard.

With his foot Paul rolled him over onto his back and rested the point of the spear lightly against the man's throat. "Talk," he said, in his best Hollywood manner. "What's this all about?"

From the mouth of Barabbas came one familiar four-letter word. Paul kicked him hard in the ribs and leaned more heavily on the spear. "Start talking or I'll have this through you."

"You wouldn't dare." The dark brown eyes gazed up contemptuously. Paul took a deep breath.

"Kill you?" he said. "No, I wouldn't do that." He moved the point of the spear an inch upwards. "But I'll have your eye out. And if you think I'm bluffing just try me." The spear came down slowly until the tip hovered over the man's right eye. "You'll have to make up your mind pretty fast."

"Piss off," said Barabbas.

Paul sighed. "Okay, go blind. It's your problem." He stabbed the spear downwards, deliberately missing the eye but cutting sharply into the man's cheek. "Damn it. Missed," he said.

"All right," Barabbas said. The contempt had gone and he was looking at Paul with horror. "You'd bloody well do it, too, wouldn't you?"

Paul said nothing. The spear was still poised at the ready.

"What do you want to know?" Barabbas asked, sullenly.

"Who put you up to this?" Paul tried a long shot. "Mandrake?"

"Who?" There was no mistaking the bewilderment in the actor's voice. "I don't know what you're talking about. Who's Mandrake?"

Again the spear made its slow, horribly steady descent. "Don't waste my time." The menace in Paul's voice surprised even himself. He'd had no idea he could sound so tough.

"No, look for God's sake! I don't know any Mandrake. I swear it! I'm not lying to you. I swear I'm not. For ... for Chrissake keep that thing away."

Wearily, Paul realised he was telling the truth. "Who was it then?"

"Huxter's old woman. His wife. She ... she put me up to it."

Paul asked: "Why?" He knew, everyone did, about there being no fury like a woman scorned but surely it was going too far, however scorned she might have been, to set this murderous man upon him. A vivid memory of that brief meeting in the hotel passed across his mind and he shuddered. "Did she say why?"

"No. Just asked me to do you over a bit."

"To kill me?"

The man shrugged. "If it worked out that way. She didn't seem too fussy. I don't think she likes you much."

"How much did she pay you?"

Barabbas looked sulky. He hesitated before replying. "She didn't give me money."

"Oh, I see. That. You come pretty cheap, don't you? Pay you in advance, did she?"

"Yeah, with a bonus to come afterwards. When I'd finished with you like."

"The joke's on her then, isn't it? You've had your fee without doing the job."

"I've also got a broken foot," the man said. "And me balls have come up the size of oranges. I've not done so bleedin' well out of it, either."

Paul threw the spear into the corner of the room and it stuck, quivering, in the wall. He went over to the door and retrieved his gun. The man lay propped up on one elbow and watched him.

"You're not going to shoot me?" he whispered.

"No. Not this time. But just don't try anything with me again. Understand?"

He went out, closing the door behind him.

The lunch break was over and they were setting up a new scene outside the temple. Roman soldiers milled around the field, Caligula and Pilate were rehearsing their lines, the director was peering through his useless viewfinder and nodding his head, sagely. Masters and Breugelhoffer were talking to Emma and Grainger, and Huxter was back on top of his ladder.

Paul avoided them all and made his way to the cluster of caravans. The one he wanted was beside Huxter's. It was long and low and painted a pale pink. Frilly, chintzy curtains hid the windows and there were deckchairs and a table set up outside under a huge sunshade.

The name on the door in blue letters was 'Anne Huxter'.

Paul went in. She was lying on the bed, reading a book. A bottle of brandy, nearly empty, and two glasses, only one of them smeared with lipstick, stood on a table beside her. Coffee steamed and bubbled in the percolator on the small, smart oil stove.

The walls of the caravan were painted lemon and hung with Goya prints. The carpet was thick and plum-coloured and the rumpled sheets on the bed matched the walls.

She leapt up when she saw him. Her thin, silk housecoat—white with a black and red dragon motif—clung contentedly to her naked body.

"What the hell!" she said.

Paul closed the door and smiled amiably upon her. "I've come to collect the bonus," he said. "Your boy's not feeling so good, so I've come in his place."

"Get out!" Her voice climbed up to screaming pitch. "Get out of here!"

He put his hand on her chest and pushed her, sprawling, back onto the bed. The housecoat fell partly open, revealing the length of one slim leg.

"Shut up," he said, "or I'll knock your front teeth out." It was his day for being tough, all right. He felt like Humphrey Bogart.

She lay still and looked him over. "What happened?"

"I won," Paul said, simply. "It was a good fight. You should have seen it."

She made an irritated clucking sound with her tongue. "I gave him too much brandy."

"Well, that, too."

She wriggled into a more comfortable position among the pillows. "What do you think you're going to do now?"

"I'm going to ask some questions," Paul said, "and you're going to answer them."

She shook her head and laughed. "I don't feel like it."

"You will." He sounded more confident than he felt.

"Make me," she said, mocking him. Just for a second he hesitated. Then he went to the percolator, poured about a quarter of a pint of steaming coffee into a cup and threw it onto her leg.

She leapt up again, squealing. An angry red blotch showed up against the whiteness of her thigh.

"That's just for a start," Paul said, his voice flat. "The next time there'll be a lot more and you'll get it in the face."

"You wouldn't dare!"

"Everyone keeps telling me that. I'd dare."

She stared at him and a look, almost of respect, came into her face. She lay back on the bed again. "I believe you would. You're a lot tougher than I took you for."

"Oh, I'm tough all right." Paul's grin was cold, more like a snarl. It felt good, in character. He wished he could see it in a mirror.

She moved onto her side so that her left hip curved up exaggeratedly, round and tight against the silk, immensely provocative. "What do you want to know?" Her voice was as silky as her dress.

He lit a cigarette, trying to maintain the calm, hard pose. "Why did you set your boy-friend onto me?"

"He's not my boy-friend. He's a nothing." She shrugged. "Someone I use occasionally, if you see what I mean."

Paul saw but let it pass. "Well?"

She laughed. "I told you it was dangerous to stand me up. Now you know just how dangerous it can be."

He stared at her, unable to believe her. "You're lying."

"All right, I'm lying." Her tongue flicked pinkly along her lower lip, leaving it moist and glistening.

He said: "It's Mandrake, isn't it? You're working for him."

Now it was her turn to stare. "Who? Darling, you're out of your little mind. I don't know any Mandrake. Honest. I just wanted to have you beaten up. I thought it all out in my own tiny brain. It seemed like a good idea because I was cross with you and I wanted you taught a lesson."

From her expression, her tone, he knew she was telling the truth. "You must be crazy," he said and opened the door to leave. Her voice stopped him, forced him to look back.

"I thought you wanted to collect the bonus," she murmured. The housecoat was fully open now. Perspiration, light as the dew on a summer morning, shone on her breasts and stomach and thighs with a curiously erotic effect.

Paul looked her over, stonily.

"You'll catch cold like that," he said and went out.

CHAPTER THIRTEEN

CONTACT

T HE BATH was deep and warm and relaxing and smelled—not too little, not too much—of a rather expensive oil from an exclusive little shop in Bond Street. As a rule, Paul did not go in much for perfumes. Indeed, if asked, he would have denied that he used them at all.

Occasionally a little discreet after-shave, Onyx by Lentheric for preference; at times a minimal use of hair-dressing by Hardy Amies; when he remembered it, a light dusting of talcum powder, Arden when he was at home but anything—even Johnson's Baby Powder—when he was staying at someone else's house.

None of these things, however, did he regard as perfumes, even less as cosmetics. They were merely aids to what the adverts called "personal freshness" and he was rather keen on that. The honest smell of manly sweat, he felt, was acceptable. But he went to considerable lengths to avoid BO or bad breath. He liked to think of himself as being nice to know.

Tonight though was a little exceptional since he had every intention of finishing it in Emma's bed. Hence the bath oil to ensure that he was not only nice to know but ravishingly desirable.

He lay back happily, watching the fragrant steam drifting up to the ceiling and letting the warm water soothe the day's aches and tensions from his body.

A cigarette was burning in the ebony holder which he only used in the bath and on the floor beside him was a large gin and tonic, heavily iced and topped with a slice of lime.

Luxury. In a little while he would be dining in an expensive restaurant with a beautiful woman. They would order only the best and he would pay for it with the nonchalance of a man who knows it's not his own money he is spending.

At times like this journalism seemed not just worthwhile but ideal. For at times like this he was living on the scale of a man who earned about five thousand a year after tax. Such interludes did not last long, nor would he want them to for after a few days of such soft living he would begin to feel flabby and fat. He would have smoked too much, eaten too heavily, drunk to excess and his present mood of sensual contentment would have changed to self-disgust.

But for the moment he was enjoying it as a man who could afford to pay for it all himself would never be able to enjoy it.

He let more hot water into the bath and thought about the events of the day.

The afternoon had passed without incident. Masters and Breugelhoffer were a little distant in their dealings with him but the grief this caused him had not been sufficient to break his heart.

The man who played Barabbas had gone back to his hotel, saying he had been knocked down by a runaway chariot, which puzzled everyone except Paul a good deal. The Lady Wife had not emerged from her caravan after Paul left her, and he had overheard Huxter explaining to Breugelhoffer that she felt unwell after spilling coffee on her leg.

"Got a nasty blister way up here on her thigh," Huxter said. "Big as a dinner plate. Poor kid."

Paul had spent most of the afternoon chatting with Emma and arranging to have some special arty pictures taken for the *Sunday Journal*, with special emphasis on Mary Magdalene's splendid charlies.

Now he felt quite virtuous. He had done what he could for both his employers. Tomorrow, when Blake got back, he might really have to start working. But until then there was tonight. And there was Emma.

He threw his cigarette end into the lavatory and climbed out of the bath, putting on the voluminous white robe supplied by the hotel and letting it soak up the water from his body.

Then he went through the whole gamut of personal freshness from the Arden to the Hardy Amies. By the time he was through he was confident that even Emma herself could hardly smell sweeter than he did.

He had dressed and was halfway through fixing his tie when the phone rang.

A man's voice said: "Mr. Baker?"

"Speaking." Paul tried to place the voice. He'd heard it before somewhere but where?

"Good," the man said. "I thought I might have missed you."

"Would that have been so terrible?" Paul asked, smiling.

"For you, perhaps. Not for me." The voice was as smug as a purr but suddenly Paul realised there was an underlying note of menace in it. He stopped smiling.

"Who is this?" he asked.

"I don't think that matters, Mr. Baker. It's what I have to say that's important."

"Then say it." The languor induced by the bath had vanished and Paul was now completely alert. He caught sight of himself in the mirror and was impressed by how alert he looked.

"Not on the phone, I think. I distrust telephones. Really, I feel we ought to meet."

Paul was silent, working it out. At first he had thought this might be Blake back from his trip but clearly it wasn't. Alternatively, it could be another of the Lady Wife's little capers designed to put him firmly in his place which, in her view, seemed to be a wooden box deep under the earth.

"Are you still there, Mr. Baker?"

"I'm here," Paul said, shortly. "I was thinking."

"A dangerous pastime sometimes. You shouldn't overindulge it. Look, I have a proposition to put to you, a lucrative one. Meet me and we'll discuss it. What have you got to lose?"

"My life?" Paul suggested. Where *had* he heard this voice before?

The man chuckled. "If I wanted to kill you, Mr. Baker, I could do it any time. There'd be no need for all this preamble. Well?"

Paul made up his mind. "Okay. Where and when?"

"Excellent. Now listen carefully. Take a taxi to the Gran Via and make a particular note of the kilometre reading as you pass the telephone exchange. It's that large building, sixteen storeys. You know it?"

"Go on."

"From there, tell the driver to turn into the Calle de la Princessa and then go out on the Segovia Road. Is that clear?"

"So far," Paul said.

"Good. Now when you have gone precisely twenty-five kilometres past the telephone exchange you will see on the right hand side of the road a bodega, a sort of bistro. The place is closed. There are shutters over the windows and no lights, so be very careful that you don't miss it.

"It's on a corner, by the way. Pay off the taxi and walk down the side street beside the bodega. About twenty yards down there's a door in the wall. It will be open. Push it and go in."

"Is that all?"

The man chuckled. "For the moment. Oh, one thing. I cannot stress too strongly the importance of your being unarmed. I urge this, I may say, for your own sake."

"I see. When must I be there?"

"The time is now 8.35. Let's say, oh, 9.45."

"Tonight?" Paul asked, anxiously. "But I have a dinner date tonight."

The voice sighed. "I know. With the delicious Miss Dane, Alas, you'll have to cancel it. This is much more important than sex, Mr. Baker."

"I hope so. It had better be. What *is* it all about, anyway?"

Again the chuckle, thick and liquid and smooth as motor oil. "Let us merely say, Mr. Baker, that it concerns the little matter of Henry Mandrake."

CHAPTER FOURTEEN

THE MAN BEHIND THE SCREEN

EIGHTEEN, nineteen, twenty … The kilometres ticked up on the clock as the taxi trundled, without undue haste, on the road to Segovia.

Paul sat in the front seat beside the driver, watching the clock. His nerves were taut and fear was getting to work on his bowels, even though, disregarding instructions, he had come armed. There was just a little comfort in the bulk of the automatic under his arm.

Despite the mystery man's reassurance, this could so easily be a trap. Some hired killer might well be waiting for him on the other side of that door in the wall. The same killer, perhaps, who had done so efficient a job on Mr. Chatham's agent, Hector Neece.

There was a thought for the day …

It was not a dangerous job, Mr. Chatham had said, and Paul in his innocence had believed him. Now he was not so sure. He was not equipped to cope with the situation in which he found himself and he felt a heavy resentment against the people that had put him there. Why me? he thought. Why me? And, while we're asking questions, where the hell is Blake? This should be his job, not mine. It's what he's paid for. I'm not trained for this kind of thing, not experienced enough and, to be perfectly frank, not brave enough.

The taxi went on. Twenty-one, twenty-two … Nearly there now. Paul looked at his watch. 9.36. Not bad timing, anyway.

The car's engine set up a whining complaint as it climbed a small hill. The driver drove as all Spanish taxi drivers seemed to do—in one gear all the time, regardless of speed, as if under the impression that you used each gear in turn until it was quite worn out and then started on the next. The whine turned to a wheeze and then to a laboured grunt.

Paul began to watch for the bodega on the right hand side of the road …

Throughout the drive he had steadfastly avoided thinking of Emma but now she came vividly to his mind. Without doubt she would be furious with him, and not without cause.

Before leaving, he had phoned her but there had been no reply. He had gone and tapped on her door. Still no reply. Finally, putting an ear to the door, he had heard, faintly, the sound of running water and above it the sound of her voice, singing.

As loudly as he dared, which was not very loud for he was scared of rousing everyone in the surrounding rooms, he had called her name but the noise of the shower had drowned him out. Emma went on singing.

In the end he had given it up. He had slipped a note under her door explaining that he had been called away on urgent business but he had little hope of her believing him. What urgent business could a visiting show business reporter have in Madrid at this time of night?

That made two women he had stood up on successive nights—a personal record. Gloomily he added Emma's name to the list of enemies he had made in the last few days. Now he had gone through the card. He couldn't think of another enemy to be made.

Twenty-three, twenty-four, twenty-fi …

"Stop," Paul said. The driver looked round, startled. Stop—here, in the middle of nowhere? He shrugged. Tourists … what could you expect?

Paul stared out. There it was, closed and unfriendly, dimly illuminated by a tired street lamp. The night was warm and still and silent. A thin, hungry cat skulked across the road but nothing else moved. It was a desolate enough spot for a rendezvous.

The driver handed over his change and Paul got out. Reluctantly. Once the car had turned and gone he would be alone to tackle God-knew-what on the other side of those shuttered windows.

He shivered slightly, despite the warmth of the night.

The appearance of the bodega was made even more forbidding by the fact that every building around it had been demolished. It stood alone and decaying in one corner of a field of rubble, like a ruin left over from the Civil War.

Paul walked over to one of the windows and tried to peer in but the shutters did their job efficiently. He could see nothing.

Neither could he hear anything. He looked around, desperate for any sign of life but even the cat had gone.

A long way in the distance, in either direction, there was the glow of car lights but he took no comfort from that. He could be struck dead here, beside the road, and the cars would pass without their occupants noticing a thing.

He lit a cigarette and turned the corner.

Exactly twenty paces down the sidestreet he came to the door. Had he not been looking for it he might easily have passed it for there were no lights here and the Iberian night was black.

He pushed the door gently and it swung open. The darkness inside was solid, impenetrable. He cursed himself for having broken his torch. Without a light even the gun, which he now had in his hand, was not all that reassuring.

For a second, standing on the threshold, he hesitated, sudden panic sending jagged shudders up his back and stiffening the hair on his neck. A desire to turn and run almost overwhelmed him. As a child he had always hated to be alone in the dark, convinced that some hideously deformed monster would spring out from the hiding places of the night and devour him.

Absurdly, he felt that fear now. "Oh, for God's sake," he muttered, aloud.

With the aid of a match he discovered that the door opened onto a narrow passage. He took a deep breath and went inside.

No monsters leaped out to devour him.

Again he paused, looking around in the light of the match. The passage smelled sourly of old, cheap wine. The walls, once white, were brown and dingy and generations of customers had scrawled their names, political slogans and the desperate obscenities of the frustrated upon them. Kilroy had been there. Franco had to go. Pedro loved Maria. Down with the Pope. Somebody's sister-in-law had fat white thighs and various other delightful attributes. The writing on the wall was the same the world over.

Heartened by this observation he went on until his way was blocked by another door. This, too, opened at a touch.

Quickly, before fear could grab him again, Paul went through, the match went out, the door closed behind him and a dim light came on in the middle of the room.

He turned and sprang back towards the door but two men were between him and it. Two men covered entirely by long black shrouds like Ku Klux Klansmen in negative. Two men with revolvers in their hands.

Paul stopped. The smaller of the two said in Spanish: "Throw the gun on the floor, turn round and keep your hands above your head."

He did all these things. Quick, deft fingers frisked him. A foot kicked his automatic across the room.

The room was long and wide and the smell of sour wine was hideously strong. In one corner was a heap of empty bottles; along one wall half a dozen broken casks.

In the centre of the room, beneath the dusty light bulb, stood a solitary chair and a few yards beyond that, a plain, dark screen.

From behind the screen a voice, the voice he had heard on the phone, said: "Good evening, Mr. Baker. The chair is for you. Please sit down."

Paul hesitated. One of the Klansmen jabbed him impatiently in the back with a gun. He sat down.

The voice that was so nearly familiar said: "Please excuse all the melodrama, Mr. Baker, but I'm afraid it wouldn't do for you to see any of us. No doubt you understand that." The last sentence was spoken with a questioning inflexion and Paul felt called upon to say something. He said: "What's this all about?"

A patient sigh drifted out to him. "Let's not waste time, Mr. Baker. You've already annoyed me by coming here armed when I specifically told you not to. Don't try me too far.

"We're here to discuss Henry Mandrake—and don't, I beg of you, pretend you don't know what I'm talking about. Obviously, you don't want to give anything away but you must realise that you haven't anything *to* give away. You know nothing that I and my associates don't."

"I don't realise anything," Paul said, stubbornly. His mouth was dry and he wanted, very badly, to get out of there. But the odds against any frantic dash for freedom seemed distinctly heavy.

One of the hooded men stood against the door, his gun pointed unwaveringly at Paul's back.

The voice said: "I intend to be reasonable, Mr. Baker. Violence will only be offered you if you insist on being stupid. Is that clear?"

Paul nodded.

"Good. Now to prove that I'm not bluffing, let me tell you some of the things I know about you. First of all, you were sent here by a certain Department in Whitehall. Your exact position with that department, I must confess, puzzles me. Your actions in Madrid have been, shall we say, unorthodox. You may, of course, be a trained agent but I rather doubt it. However, that's really beside the point. The main thing is that you are here in connection with the sale by Henry Mandrake of certain information to the Russians."

Paul said: "How do you know these things?"

"Well, I knew—because a certain Hector Neece, rather against his will I must add in all fairness, told us so—that someone from your department would be coming here. The fact that I knew that person to be you is entirely your own fault. You've made a lot of mistakes, Mr. Baker."

"Obviously," Paul said.

"There was one grave error in particular that identified you to us very early on. Still, we are extremely thorough. We checked all other possible suspects before we approached you this evening. We had to be perfectly certain of your identity, you see. And we were."

Paul said: "So it was one of your people I met in Miss Dane's room?"

"That's right. The same man who talked to Neece, actually. However. Let me make my position clear. Your presence in Spain is a nuisance to us. At the risk of offending you, I must add that it's not much more than that. Nevertheless, you will have to be eliminated."

The voice laughed. "I'm sorry. I see I frightened you. In circumstances like these I suppose the word eliminated *is* rather sinister. However, I don't intend to have you killed …"

"Thank you," Paul said, meaning it. Nothing, he was aware, would be easier for the man behind the screen than to have him murdered here and now.

"… unless it proves necessary," the voice continued. "My leniency is due to the fact that the death, or even disappearance, of an Englishman in Madrid would lead to the involvement of the police and the British Embassy and that is something I should like to avoid if possible. Fortunately, there is a way to eliminate you as a source of possible danger without doing anything drastic."

The man at the door yawned loudly and shifted his gun from one hand to the other. Neither he nor the second hooded man seemed interested in the conversation.

Paul wriggled uncomfortably in his chair. The sweat was making his clothes stick to his body.

The voice said: "Do you remember what you did on your first night in Madrid?"

"I got drunk."

"Indeed you did. But do you remember anything else?"

"There wasn't anything else," Paul said, blustering. Anything could have happened that night.

"Alas for you, something else did happen, though I'm not surprised that you've forgotten it."

"If it did I must have been drugged."

The man behind the screen laughed quietly. "Not drugged exactly. Let's just say that you were helped on your way to the rather disgusting state in which you finished the night."

"So what happened?" Paul said.

"That I'd rather not tell you. But *something* happened, believe me. I have certain evidence which, if it got into the hands of the head of your department, would discredit you for ever. For your own sake, I urge you to believe that."

Paul did believe him. The man's voice simply oozed sincerity. He said: "What do you intend to do with this ... evidence?"

"Nothing—so long as you are sensible. Within the next few days Mandrake and the Russians will have completed their deal. Nothing will be allowed to interfere with that because, one way and another, around £200,000 is about to change hands. Now that's a good deal of money, Mr. Baker. To make that kind of money you can safely assume that my associates and I would do practically anything."

From behind the screen came the sound of water being poured into a glass. The owner of the voice was thirsty. He had been doing a lot of talking.

"So my proposition is this: for the next few days you will sit back and enjoy your stay in Madrid. Nothing else. If your department wishes to know what is happening you will report failure. You will tell them, in fact, that you have reason to believe that Mandrake has left Spain.

"In return, I shall, on the day you leave for London, deliver to you one thousand pounds in sterling. I shall also destroy—and you have my word for this—the evidence I mentioned earlier. You understand?"

"Yes," Paul said. "But ..."

"But if you don't do as I suggest," the voice went on, smooth and even as ever, "the evidence will be sent to London and to certain other people and you will be killed."

"If you're going to kill me anyway," Paul said, "why bother sending the evidence?"

"A personal whim. I like to think of you dying in disgrace."

"Not even the consolation of a hero's death?"

"Certainly not."

"Not much of a choice then, is it?"

"No, I suppose not. However, I shall give you time to think it over. If I demanded an answer now, in these rather intimidating surroundings, you might be tempted to deceive me. Better, I think, for you to go away and consider the position carefully and coolly.

"After all, it's quite simple. On the one hand, a pleasant stay in a luxury hotel with the delightful Miss Dane to hold your hand, a thousand pounds to ease your conscience—and your life. On the other hand, death and dishonour. Think about it, Mr. Baker. I shall telephone tomorrow for your answer—an affirmative one, I have little doubt. In the meantime ..."

In the meantime, the hooded men moved swiftly to Paul's side and, before he could struggle or even protest, had each grabbed one of his arms.

"I hate to have to do this," said the voice. "But I want to be quite sure that you don't attempt to follow us."

With sudden violence the barrel of a gun smashed down on the back of Paul's head.

CHAPTER FIFTEEN

LA NOTTEE

WHEN he came to, the room was empty and in darkness. He was lying, face down, on the floor and his head, from the top of his skull to the base of his neck, ached horribly. Even the slight movement he made, nothing more than a stirring of the limbs, as consciousness returned, was enough to make him cry out.

He lay as still as possible until the throbbing in his head eased a little. Then, groaning, he staggered up.

"The bastards," he said.

Leaning against his chair for support he lit a match. In its brief glare he saw his automatic, still lying against the wall. Fat lot of good that had been. He bent, grunting with pain, to pick it up and then, with more matches to guide him, found his way out and into the street.

There, giddy and exhausted, he clung like a cartoon drunk to the nearest lamp-post while he waited for a taxi to come by. In that deserted spot he waited a long time.

Meanwhile, he made an inventory of the damage he had suffered. Basically, it amounted to a splitting headache and a large lump on his skull.

His watch was still going, though the glass had been cracked in his fall. His suit was crumpled and dusty and his shirt front was a mess. Otherwise he seemed to be intact.

The time by the watch was 11.45 which meant he had been in the bodega for the best part of two hours. As far as he could estimate he must have been unconscious about half that time, so the three men would be miles away by now. Again he wondered about the voice but he could put neither name nor face to it.

The night air, cooler now, eased his headache and he started thinking clearly again. What he thought about was the proposition that had been put to him and the more he thought about it the more furious he became.

It wasn't simply the bump on his head, though it would have taken an even bigger coward than Paul considered himself to be to accept that meekly. It was more the contempt with which he had been treated that night that enraged him.

A nuisance, that was all they thought him. An irritant to be scratched away with a thousand lousy quid—one two-hundredth part of the loot that would change hands when the deal was done.

Well, to hell with them. They'd soon see what a mistake that was.

Cars passed by and he stepped out into the road to thumb a lift but nobody stopped. The fact that Paul himself would not have stopped for a dusty, dishevelled hitch-hiker in this place at this time of night did not prevent him from cursing them obscenely as they sped past.

It was after midnight before an empty cab came into sight. And by then Paul knew what he must do next.

Everything seemed to hinge around what had happened the night he got so drunk. Therefore if he could discover just what did happen and who made it happen he would be, if not ahead of the voice and his associates, at least in step with them.

And to do that he must find the girl he had been with that night. Rosemary. That was her name. Memory stopped with her but perhaps she could fill him in on the rest.

The taxi stopped as he signalled and the driver peered out cautiously. Paul waved banknotes around to reassure him and got in.

"Do you know a place called La Nottee?" he asked.

"Si, senor."

"Take me there."

"Si, senor. But I know a much better place where the girls are cheaper and cleaner. Twelve hundred pesetas for the whole night. A lovely place, senor. Much …"

"La Nottee," Paul said, firmly.

"Si, senor." The taxi moved off, howling in first gear, towards Madrid.

Paul brushed himself down as best he could and sat back, head throbbing still, and thought about Emma. Too late now to phone and apologise for walking out on her. Besides, what could he say? That he had been beaten up in a deserted pub twenty-odd kilometres outside the city? A likely tale indeed.

He wondered what she had done, once she discovered she had been abandoned for the night. Gone out most likely with someone else. Grainger probably. The reflection brought a fresh onset of gloom.

"Damn," he said. "Damn, damn, damn."

The cab pulled up in a quiet, prosperous-looking street not far from the Prado art gallery.

There were few people about and the building before which they stopped was a tall, dignified kind of place that might have contained expensive flats or the offices of some well-established firm of solicitors. Few lights showed from anywhere within and there was no sound of music or revelry.

"I wanted La Nottee," Paul said. "It's a night club."

The driver nodded. "This is it, senor. In the basement." He leaned over the seat to give directions. "You go through the main doors and down the steps on the other side of the vestibule. Turn right along the corridor and you come to a pink door. That is La Nottee."

Paul tossed a handful of notes to him and got out. He went through the main doors and down the stairs. None of it was familiar to him. He had no sense of ever having been there before.

When he got to the pink door, he paused. Maybe this was not the place after all. He only had Emma's word for it that he had been to La Nottee and how did she know? She hadn't been there. Or had she?

While he hesitated, the pink door opened, letting out first a burst of dance music and the sound of laughter and, secondly, two Americans, both about forty and almost identical in appearance—Madison Avenue from their black-framed executive-type glasses down to their Brooks Brother suits and their expensive black shoes.

They were both also extremely drunk but only one of them seemed happy about it.

The happy one lurched and fell against Paul as he came out and clung to him for support. "Sorry, feller. Very sorry. Helluva slippery carpet."

Paul released himself from the joyous embrace. "That's all right."

The happy drunk fell back against the wall. "I want you to know that I jus' had the bes' goddamn lay I've had in six years. But the bes' ..."

"Rosemary?" Paul asked. It was a long shot and like most long shots it didn't come off.

"Rosemary? Who th' hell's Rosemary? Mariella—tha's the girl. Bes' lay I've had in six years."

"You're crazy," said the other, lugubrious, drunk. "You probably got the clap already." The thought seemed to give him a certain grim pleasure.

The happy one laughed. "Don' lissen to him. He's a killjoy. 'Sa great place this. Beauriful girls. My name's Chuck," he said, with an abrupt change of subject. "Who're you?"

"Paul," said Paul.

"Hall? What Hall?"

"Albert Hall," Paul said. It was the first thing that occurred to him.

"Kinda familiar," said Chuck. "Heard it before."

"I'm well known in London."

"Sure! Sure, I've hearda you. Hey, Charlie, you know who this is? This is Albert Hall. He's well-known in London."

"Yeah," said Charlie, sourly. He was propped up against the door with a sneer on his face. "I know his reputation. It stinks."

Chuck put a heavy arm around Paul's shoulder. "Don' lissen to him. He's a killjoy. Hey, why'n't you come on in, Albert? Le's have a drink."

Paul allowed himself to be hustled in to a small lobby that blossomed into a discreetly lit bar. The carpet was black and the walls were papered in red and white Regency stripes. Crystal chandeliers hung from the ceiling. Still the place was unfamiliar to him.

Chuck led him over to the bar with the truculent Charlie swaying and grumbling in the rear.

"You come on with me," Chuck said, in a confidential shout, "and I'll in'roduce you to the sweetest little lay you ever had. Bes' lay I've had in six years."

"Best nothing," said Charlie. He aimed soda at his whisky and it splashed onto his knees. He hardly seemed to notice it but carried on squirting till the water ran down his legs. Paul watched, fascinated. "I had better times giving myself one off the wrist."

"Well," said Paul, gently removing the syphon. "You do lend to meet a nicer kind of person that way." He had no idea what he was talking about but he could not bear to see the man soaking himself in soda water any longer. Anyway, some of the stuff had splashed onto him.

"You hear that, Charlie?" demanded Chuck. "You hear what Albert says? He talks a lotta sense, you gotta admit that."

Charlie snatched the syphon back and squirted it wildly into a bowl of peanuts. "He talks a lotta bulldust. He talks more bull-dust than you do."

The bar led off into a larger room where a small band played and couples swayed together on a tiny dance floor. A dozen or so tables were scattered around and, at some of them women sat alone waiting to be be picked up. They were mostly young, over made-up and under-dressed. The men tended to be middle-aged and smelling highly of money.

Three of the walls were covered with red and black striped wallpaper. The fourth was decorated with obscene murals in which girls with impossible figures were doing unlikely things to men of improbable development. All very "nottee" indeed.

Chuck led them over to one of the tables, sat down and summoned a waiter who took their order and went away to a smaller bar at the far end of the room.

Paul looked around, wondering which of the girls, if any, was Rosemary. He had no recollection of what she looked like but merely hoped that he would recognise her if he saw her.

Four women gave him the come-on sign but none of them touched any chord of memory.

The waiter came back with drinks and Chuck and Charlie fell into a torrid argument over the merits of a brunette in a tight red dress, whom both seemed to know rather intimately. It was apparent that they spent a good deal of time here.

Paul was glad to be with them. He would have been conspicuous by himself and that could have been a mistake. If something had happened that first night in Spain it must have happened here. He could remember, at least in outline, most of what had taken place in the other bars they had visited. It was from here on, always assuming that La Nottee was indeed the right place, that memory broke down.

So until he could discover what it was all about, it was better to be anonymous, to appear to be a randy pleasure-seeker on a night out. For all he knew, the three men he had been with that night might be here now, watching for him. If they were, they would hardly expect to find him in the company of a couple of drunken Americans.

"Hey," said Charlie, suddenly. "There goes Mariella. See?"

Paul looked and saw, for the first time, a small flight of stairs leading up to a tiny landing and a plain white door. Memory rushed back. He remembered those stairs and that door. And he remembered, too, a blonde woman, plumpish, fortyish in a tight silver dress. Swiftly, his eyes searched the crowd, seeking for her.

A girl was going up the stairs and a man was stumbling after her intent apparently on biting her bottom. The girl was dark and slim.

"Mariella," said Chuck. His voice was tragic. "With another feller. She said she'd save herself for me."

"I toldja," Charlie said, savagely. "I toldja she was no good."

"Bes' lay I've had in six years."

"Whadda you know?" Charlie asked. "From nothing, that's what you know. You can't even lay your wife."

"Whadda you mean?"

"She told me."

"Whadda you know 'bout my wife?"

"I've laid your wife. I've laid her plenty."

"You're a liar …"

There she was! Over at the bar. Blonde, plumpish, forty-ish, just as he remembered. Paul got up softly and left the table. Neither man noticed him go.

Rosemary was sitting on a bar stool, chin propped on one hand, a glass of Coca-Cola in front of her. She looked tired.

Paul sat beside her. "Hello, Rosemary," he said, quietly.

She turned, and any left-over doubt about her identity vanished at once. Recognition and fear came into her eyes simultaneously. He felt a little thrill of excitement. He had been right. It *had* happened here. And she was the one who could tell him about it.

"I'm sorry," she said, in Spanish. "I don't know you."

"Yes, you do Rosemary. You know me well. We went to bed together."

She started to get up but he seized her arm, his fingers digging harshly into her soft flesh. "Don't go away."

"You're hurting me." But she sat still, making no further attempt to leave.

Paul took out his wallet and opened it, showing the wad of notes and travellers' cheques in the money compartment. "Some of this is for you—if you're nice. If not, I *will* hurt you." He put on his tough expression and stared at her, unblinking and menacing. He was getting good at it with all the practice he had had that day.

"What do you want?" she asked.

"Just tell me what happened the other night."

"Nothing happened." But she looked away as she said it and he noticed that she was trembling.

"Don't be frightened," he said, gently. "I won't harm you if you tell me the truth."

"You!" Her face was full of contempt. "I'm not afraid of you."

Paul dropped the gentle approach. He grabbed her arm again and squeezed it hard, just above the elbow, watching her wince as his fingers pressed against the bone. "Then maybe you should be."

"Let go," she said. "Please. I can't tell you anything. I swear it. I can't tell you anything."

He squeezed harder still, hating himself for doing it. She drew in breath sharply as the pain increased. "Let me go," she said again. "Or I'll have you thrown out of here."

He laughed. "Sure. Who by?"

"Look around you. Look at the waiters."

He looked—and suddenly realised how large they all were and how many cauliflower ears and flattened noses they had between them. "Bouncers?" he asked.

She nodded. "Now will you let me go?"

Paul released her arm. "All right. But I think you're a fool."

She shrugged and said, not unkindly: "Perhaps. But so are you. Listen to me. Go away. Forget what happened here. It will be better for you in the end, believe me."

He looked at her and smiled. "You could be right. I'll go back to my table."

"No." She shook her head. "You must leave here. Now. Otherwise ..." She glanced pointedly towards the bouncers.

Paul climbed off his stool. "Since you put it like that ..." He laid a thousand peseta note on the bar in front of her. "Buy yourself a drink for old times' sake," he said and turned away.

Larry Grainger was going up the stairs towards the white door.

Paul stopped, wondering whether to follow him. Rosemary said: "Do you need an escort?"

He looked back, over his shoulder. "I can find my own way." Without glancing again in Grainger's direction he walked away. As he passed his table he stopped, briefly. Chuck was sitting there alone. He looked as if he had been crying.

"Where's Charlie?" Paul asked.

"There." Chuck gestured towards the dance floor, where Charlie was wrapped round a large redhead. "The bastard laid my wife." Large tears wobbled down Chuck's face.

"I know," Paul said. He felt a surge of pity for the man. "Why don't you get out of here. Leave him."

"I can't do that. He's my frien'. We were at college together. I can't just walk out on him."

Paul left him. On the way out he stopped a waiter and asked what time the place closed.

"Three-thirty, senor."

It was gone two now. Paul said: "Do the girls live here? Do they stay the night?"

"No, senor. They leave at three-thirty. Sometimes one may go out alone and then you can make an arrangement with her. It is cheaper then."

"Thanks."

He went out, through the pink door, up the stairs and into the street. Nobody was around. He crossed the road and went up the steps to the porch of the house opposite. It was dark there and, sitting in the corner, he could watch the people coming out of La Nottee without being seen himself. He lit a cigarette and waited.

Time passed slowly. His throat and mouth were dry from the smoky heat of the night club and he longed for a cold beer. He was hungry, too. He had not eaten since that morning and his stomach was sending out rumbling messages of protest.

Two-forty. He felt tired and grubby and his head still hurt. He wriggled uncomfortably on the hard stone step and lit another cigarette.

Soon after three the people began to come out, first singly or in pairs, then groups of them together. Taxis emerged from nowhere and hung around for fares.

Chuck came out alone, looking sad and sober and somehow a lot older than when Paul had met him in the corridor. Ten minutes later Charlie appeared with his arm round a girl. Mariella. It really hadn't been Chuck's night at all.

At 3.25 the flow of people and traffic dwindled. Still Rosemary had not appeared. Three-thirty slipped by. Paul ground out his fourth cigarette in an hour and waited on.

By 3.40 the taxis stopped coming and he began to wonder whether he had missed her. He swore quietly and decided to give up for the night.

And then he saw her. She was arm-in-arm with a short, elderly man in a dinner jacket, who staggered a little and kept reaching up to nibble her ear. She bore it stoically, smiling her mechanical, professional smile and guided his erratic footsteps in the direction she wanted to go.

Paul waited till they were a hundred yards away and then followed. They didn't notice him.

After a while they turned down a side street and Paul broke into a run, moving silently as he covered the ground between himself and them. He was up with them before they knew it.

Rosemary gave a little shriek as she recognised him.

The man said: "What do you want?" and tried to look stern and tough. It was a hopeless task for a man of his age and build.

"Go home," Paul said. "Go on—back to your wife and kids."

"How dare you ..."

Paul made a move towards him and the man retreated, not looking stern or tough at all. "Very well. Very well." He scuttled away, without looking back.

Paul said, pleasantly: "Well, Rosemary. So now we're alone. Just you and me. So let's have a nice, quiet little cha ..."

Something heavy, something that felt like a cosh, hit him on the back of the head and somebody doused the moon and stars. His face hit the pavement with a squashy sound and dimly, a long way off it seemed, he heard someone scream.

And then the world was silent.

It stayed that way for several minutes and the first thing he heard when his senses unscrambled themselves was a car disappearing fast into the distance.

He struggled up, groaning, and once more examined himself for damage. His head ached worse than ever, his shirt front had got a little dirtier and, unaccountably, his suit reeked of brandy, as if he had bathed in it.

Cheap brandy at that. His nose wrinkled in disgust at the powerful fumes. Whoever had splashed the stuff on him might have used Carlos Primero or Fundador instead of this fire-water ...

He wiped his face on his sleeve and looked about him ...

Rosemary was lying on the pavement nearby, her clothing ripped from neck to groin and her eyes staring, wide and unblinking, at the night sky. The handle of a knife protruded from her left breast. Unfamiliar though he was with the look of death, Paul could tell a corpse when he saw one.

He lit a cigarette with hands that shook and leaned back against the wall, waiting for the pain in his head to ease.

As he sucked down the fourth lungful of smoke he became aware of another car, also going very fast but with a significant difference. This one was not going away. It was coming towards him.

At once the warning bells sounded in his mind.

The men from the bodega *had* been at La Nottee tonight. Watching out for him, perhaps, or keeping an eye on Rosemary. And when Paul followed her, they had followed him. And now she was dead.

And in that fast approaching car would be ... the police. It had to be. Because that would explain a lot: like the ripped dress and the brandy; like why he had been left unconscious beside the body. It was a safe bet that a few minutes ago an anonymous someone had phoned the nearest police station, telling of ... what? A scream in the night, maybe. A row between a man and a woman. A suspicion that someone was being murdered.

And it might have worked. If Paul had remained unconscious a little longer, the police would have found him here, apparently drunk and stinking of booze, his guilt plain for all to see. And the man behind the screen would have had no need to worry about him any more.

But as it was ...

The car was getting rapidly closer, too damn close. Paul set off at a run down the street, away from the sound.

But then ... the knife! A hundred to one his fingerprints were on it. He raced back, fumbling with a handkerchief to wipe the handle clean.

At the top of the street, the advance flash of approaching headlights cut chunks out of the night.

Frantically, he wiped the knife and his stomach convulsed as his clumsy fingers drove the blade in deeper. Then he turned and was away, running like a man trying to qualify for the Olympics.

Behind him the police car rounded the corner, screaming down to where the body lay. Paul skidded left into a darker, narrower street and clung to the wall as he struggled to pump air into his burning lungs.

A quick glance back at the car showed two men on their knees beside Rosemary and two others walking slowly in his direction, shining torches into every doorway.

He started running again, softly, on the balls of his feet and did not stop until he was a mile away from there.

By the time he got back to the hotel he was sweating, filthy and exhausted.

In that condition he dared not use the main entrance and risk being seen by the night porter. Instead he went to the back of the building where the fire escape was, climbed it to the second floor and after a lot of fumbling and cursing managed to force a window and scramble into the corridor.

One problem still remained—how to get into his room. The door was locked and he had no key. And while opening the window had been comparatively easy, he had no idea how to force a bedroom door.

He took a deep breath, rapped sharply on Emma's door and prayed that she was a light sleeper.

He was in luck. Almost at once he heard a mumbled "Whossat?" He knocked again and in a moment the door opened and there she was, blinking in the light.

She wore a black nylon négligé with frills on the cuffs and a collar that buttoned high up on the neck. The light material clung to her body and she gave off a warm, exciting smell of scent and sleep. "Hello," he said. His grin was ingratiating, hopeful rather than confident.

She looked him over bleakly. "Isn't it a little late for dinner, Mr. Baker? By my watch it's nearly five in the morning. Or are you asking me out to breakfast? If you are, I'm afraid it's a little early for me."

"No sarcasm," he said. "Please. I couldn't stand it."

The frosty blue eyes examined him with loathing. "God, just look at you. What a mess ... and the smell! I suppose you've been out with the girls again. They play rough around here, don't they? I wonder what you can have done to make a whore punch you on the nose."

"It wasn't like that. Honestly, I ..."

"Oh? What was it then—sales time at the cat-house? Cut rates for regular customers? Or were they giving out Green Shield Stamps tonight?"

"Please. I ... I ..." The long day, the lack of food, the tension and the beatings all caught up with him at once and his legs seemed no longer able to support him. He fell against the door, knocking her back into the room as he collapsed, dizzily, on the carpet.

"You drunken ..." And then she stopped. Despite his appearance and the stink of brandy, she realised that he was not drunk at all. She watched him wonderingly as he got up.

"I'm sorry." He grinned at her, embarrassed. "I'd like to explain but I can't. I mustn't. I ... look, if you want me to get out I'll go. But I'd be grateful if you wouldn't mention any of this to anyone."

She thought it over. Then ... "Don't just stand there. Come on in." She ushered him into the bedroom, closed the door and poured him a large whisky from the bottle that still had J. J. Huxter's compliments attached to it.

As she went briskly about this business, Paul watched and wondered, as he had done often in the last couple of days. Friend or foe? How could he tell?

"Halt," he murmured. "Who goes there?"

"What?"

He sighed. "Nothing." Even to himself he sounded desperately tired.

She sat in the arm-chair and crossed her legs, and their shape was clearly visible beneath the nylon. He sighed again. Here he was in her bedroom; she was practically undressed and yet he was as far away from her as ever.

"Can I ask you any questions?" she said. He shook his head. "Well, can I ask you this—why did you knock on my door? I presume it wasn't to see if you could get into bed with me?"

"No. Tonight I wanted a different favour. I wondered if I could use your balcony to get into my room."

She stared and then laughed. "This is ridiculous."

"I know. But I haven't got my key and, for various reasons, I don't want to ask the night man for it. So the only way I can get to bed is by way of your balcony."

"Do you think you can manage it?" She looked dubious. "You look just about whacked to me."

"I can manage it."

She waved a hand towards the window. "Then be my guest."

He finished his whisky and stood up. "Thanks. One day, I'd like to …"

"Shut up," she murmured. For a second the blue eyes were soft and warm. "Go to bed."

He climbed onto the ledge of the balcony and poised himself for the short leap across.

"Batman flies again," she said.

CHAPTER SIXTEEN

INCRIMINATING EVIDENCE

THE sound of the curtains being pulled back from the windows woke him up and he groaned and rolled over, opening one eye. Josef's nephew Miguel, was standing beside the bed with a tray in his hands.

"Wha ..." Paul blinked the sleep out of his eyes. "I didn't order breakfast."

"No, senor. Mr. Masters told me to bring it."

"Mr. Masters? What the hell ... what time is it?"

"Five past nine, senor." Miguel gazed down at him with the bland inscrutability of the hotel waiter, the man who sees all, hears all and—assuming he is tipped generously enough—says nothing.

"Oh, Christ." Paul sat up, stiffly. He had had barely four hours sleep and it wasn't enough. Not nearly enough. Damn Neddy Masters.

"Well, leave the bloody tray now it's here," he said, irritably.

"Si, senor." Miguel set the tray down soundlessly on the table. There was coffee, hot rolls, a dish of ham and eggs. Paul looked at it with surprise. What was this for? Why the full English breakfast?

Miguel glided over to the door. "Mr. Masters said he would call in half an hour, senor. He hoped you would be dressed by then."

"What!" Paul said but the waiter had gone.

Paul shrugged. He would know what it was all about soon enough. Meanwhile he was starving. Grunting a little, he reached out greedily for the bacon and eggs.

By a quarter to ten, when Masters came in, Paul had eaten, showered and dressed and lit his first cigarette of the day. Apart from a sore head and a tiredness that was like a mild hangover he didn't feel at all bad.

"Thanks for the breakfast," he said.

"That's all right." Masters stood by the door. He looked awkward, embarrassed.

"Well?" Paul said. "What's up?"

Masters said: "I don't know how to say it." He walked over to the window and looked out at the sharp, hard lines of the city. "I just don't know where to start. Oh, damn Huxter." His voice rose petulantly. "Why did he have to pick on me?"

Paul leaned against the dressing-table and blew out a pale stream of smoke. "Well?" he said again. "Go on. Whatever it is, say it. I'm a big boy. I can take it."

Masters' voice was carefully controlled, very quiet. "I've come to tell you to leave."

"What?"

"It's Huxter, you see. He … he's withdrawn your invitation." Masters took a deep breath. "He's had you booked on the next plane and I've been sent to make sure you catch it."

There was silence and then Paul laughed. "You're joking, of course?"

"No."

"But why? I mean, for Pete's sake, what have I done?"

Masters turned abruptly and looked at Paul as if seeing him for the first time. His expression was not entirely friendly. "It's because of this." He held out an envelope.

"What is it?"

"I think you know."

Paul opened it. Inside there was a photograph, six inches by four, of a man and a woman on a bed. They were naked and the scene was like the highlight of a particularly blue film, for what they were doing to each other was unbelievably obscene. Their bodies were slightly out of focus as if they had been moving when the picture was taken, but the faces were clear and recognisable. The girl was Rosemary. The man was himself. "I don't believe it," Paul said, softly. "I just don't believe it."

It couldn't be. Not him. Not doing this. No matter how drunk he had been.

"It's a fake. It's just not true."

Masters shrugged. "You know what they say, old boy. The camera doesn't lie."

"But … where did you get it?"

"It was shoved under the door of the Huxters' suite, addressed to the Lady Wife, some time after midnight."

Paul shook his head, as if the physical action might throw his wits back into some semblance of working order. "But who sent it?"

"Don't you know?" Masters grinned faintly. "Look on the back."

Paul turned the picture over. The message on the back said: "Thinking of you. Love, Paul."

"It's not my writing," he said but he knew that it was similar enough. "I didn't send this."

"Oh, come on!" Masters was edgy with impatience.

But surely you don't believe …"

"Paul, it doesn't matter what I believe but if you want to know, I … well, I imagine you got drunk again and thought the picture would give everyone a big laugh. How the hell do I know?"

A suspicion, horrifying in its implications, crept into Paul's mind. "Who else got one of these?"

"Emma. That's all. Well, you must know that."

That's *all*? Only Emma? "Dear God," Paul said. He sat down heavily on the bed.

Masters looked at his watch. "Anyway, I've to get you to the airport within an hour. You'd better start packing."

Paul stared again at the picture in his hand. However it had been managed, that was him all right in that revolting pose. There was no arguing against that. And yet it was a fake, something rigged up while he lay drunk and unaware of what was happening. "Listen," he said. "I'm not leaving. Huxter can do as he likes but I'm staying here. I'll pay for the room myself. I'll …

"You'll get the hell out of here!" Paul swung round as the new voice yelled across the room. Huxter was standing at the door, looking and sounding furious. "You'll get out of this goddam hotel. You scum!"

"Now, look here," Paul's own temper rose to boiling point. But Huxter cut in on him.

"You be out of here in twenty minutes or, by God, I'll have you arrested. And if you think I can't, if you think I'm spending all that dough in this lousy country without having one hell of a pull with the police, just stick around and see what happens. By Christ, I'll have you in a cell before you can holler 'Help!'"

Masters moved across and placed himself, diplomatically, between Paul and Huxter. "He can do it, Paul. Look, cut your losses. Get out before you do something we all might be sorry about."

Paul said, his voice wild with anger: "I'm not going to let that fat little …"

"Watch it, feller!" Rage had turned Huxter's face dangerously scarlet. "You just watch it! In my book you're a degenerate and a pervert. So you just get your arse out of this country and don't ever come near me again or, by God, I'll ..."

A look of mingled pain and horror showed suddenly in his eyes. He clutched his chest and reeled sideways against the door jamb. "My heart! Oh, God, my heart! Neddy, quick ..."

He lurched out into the corridor and Masters, bounding after him, said: "Paul, be ready in twenty minutes, for heaven's sake."

And then Paul was alone. He sat down again, all the strength gone from his legs, his mind a crazy kaleidoscope of disjointed thoughts and theories.

When he glanced up, Emma was standing by the door. For a moment they just looked at each other. Then she said: "That was a rotten thing you did." Her voice was low, as if she had difficulty controlling it. Her lips were trembling and she looked pale and very lovely. He stared across at her, unable to speak, unable to think of anything to say.

"I can't think ... I mean, I can't ... I can't see what you were trying to prove." From the pocket of her trim, white skirt she produced a tiny handkerchief and used it to wipe her eyes. "Why did you do it?"

Paul rubbed a hand wearily across his mouth. "You believe I sent you that picture?"

"I don't know. What else can I think?" The look she gave him was filled with anguish. "Oh, Paul, I don't know. It ... it's such a bloody horrible picture."

He said: "Emma, believe me, I didn't know anything about it until a few minutes ago. I swear it. It's a phoney. A frame-up. I want you to believe that. I don't care what anybody else believes but ..."

The self-control, so carefully imposed, gave way. Tears showed in her eyes, she made an oddly touching, choking sound in her throat and then she rushed into her room, slamming the door behind her.

Paul stood up, feeling heavy and old and tired, to get another cigarette.

Beside him the phone rang and when he lifted the receiver the voice he knew but could not place said. "Ah, Mr. Baker, I imagine by now you know I wasn't bluffing."

"I know," Paul said, dully. "You sent the pictures."

"Correct. I also sent one back to your Department. What kind of reaction do you think it will get there?" The voice chuckled—a joyous, fruity sound. "Well, Mr. Baker, do you realise what you've done? You're very foolish, you know, very foolish indeed. Not only are you quite dishonoured but a young woman has been killed, simply because you would disregard my warning. There's a thought for you. A death, utterly unnecessary, on your conscience. Poor Mr. Baker. Poor, silly Mr. Baker." There was a click of a receiver being replaced and the line went dead.

Paul hung up. It had been obvious enough where the photographs had come from but it was something at least to know for sure.

Well, he had been aware of the odds when he went to La Nottee last night and if the gamble had failed there was no point in complaining. He was sorry for Rosemary but he could not feel responsibility for her death. She had conspired with others against him and if they had turned against her, that was the risk she had run, a risk she must have known about.

It occurred to him that the man on the phone had not said anything about having him killed, too. Perhaps they weren't going to bother now. They'd have to be quick, anyway, because …

No, by God, they wouldn't have to be quick. Because, whatever Huxter might think, Paul was not leaving Madrid. He *had* to stay—to find out who had taken those pictures. Otherwise there would be a number of people he could never face again, Mr. Chatham being only one of them and not, at present in any event, the most important.

Quickly, he locked his bedroom door and began to pack. Most of his belongings he threw into his suitcase. Into his overnight bag went a couple of shirts, socks, handkerchiefs, underwear and toilet accessories.

From the secret compartment in his typewriter he took his automatic and slipped it into the shoulder holster. The other gun he put into the pouch pocket in his trousers.

He had just finished fastening his zip when Masters came back. Miguel was with him.

"Ready?"

"Ready."

Miguel took the case and typewriter and Paul carried his overnight bag himself.

The three of them trooped down the corridor in single file, Masters leading and Miguel, Paul noted with sour amusement, bringing up the rear. This, presumably so that one of them could stop him if he tried anything outlandish on the way.

Josef was standing outside his room, next to the Huxters' suite, as the little procession went by. He looked at Paul gravely and not without sympathy. "You are leaving, senor?"

"That's right. I know when I'm not wanted."

"I am sorry, senor. Very sorry." Josef hesitated, then held out his hand. Touched, Paul grasped it. "Thank you," he said.

Impulsively, he took out the envelope with the twenty pounds that Huxter had left in his room and gave it to Josef.

"Get yourself a piece of tail," he said. "With Mr. Huxter's compliments."

In the lift Masters said: "Good job J.J. didn't see you do that. He'd have just about burst."

"Yes? How is he?"

"All right. He gets heart flutters, that's all. He'll live."

"Pity."

A black Mercedes was waiting outside the main entrance. Miguel put Paul's luggage in the back and Masters climbed in behind the steering wheel. Paul got in beside him.

Neither spoke as the car headed out towards the airport. The morning's events had erected a wall between them which words were powerless to destroy. Masters concentrated on his driving and Paul sat back, apparently bored, but in fact watching out for the opportunity he sought.

It came as the car stopped at a light. Across the road three cabs waited on a taxi rank. Paul said: "Mind waiting while I get some cigarettes?"

"I've got plenty." Masters fumbled in his pocket and produced a flip-top packet.

"I want filters."

"All right, then. Hurry up."

Paul opened the car door and then, as Masters glanced up at the traffic light, knelt on the seat and poised himself.

"Sorry, Ned," he murmured and hit him hard under the ear with a perfectly timed right hook. Masters grunted and slumped across the steering wheel.

Paul grabbed his overnight bag and ran across the road to the first of the waiting cabs. "The Gran Via." he said. "I'll tell you when to stop." Through the back window, he saw Masters get out of the Mercedes, holding a hand to his ear, and looking wildly around him. Paul ducked down out of sight.

When he looked up again, Masters was walking towards a café. To telephone, no doubt. To warn the anxious world that the wild and degenerate Baker was at large. Lock up your daughters. Hide away your wife. Sexy Baker is on the prowl.

Paul stopped the taxi near the telephone exchange and walked the rest of the way. The narrow street was busier today, crowded with shoppers. Outside the café across the road half a dozen men smoked and drank.

The boutique, however, was empty and Paul went in and rapped on the counter, hoping the supercilious young man would not emerge from the curtained quarters at the back. He did not. In his place came a slight, middle-aged man with rimless glasses and hair that lay flat across his head as if it was simply too tired to lie any other way.

"Mr. Blake?"

"Yes. Can I help you?"

Paul lowered his eyes. He was suddenly self-conscious, now that he had to go through the furtive, schoolboy business of repeating the identification code.

"Mr. Arthur sends his regards," he muttered.

"How kind of him. I hope he's well."

"Yes. But his wife is ill."

"I *am* sad. Nothing serious, I trust?"

"The usual trouble." (Now what exactly did *that* mean?)

They shook hands.

"Paul Baker?"

"Yes. Can we talk?"

"Well, not just now." Blake gestured towards the curtain. "My assistant is in there. He doesn't know about the Department."

"I see." Paul was disappointed. "I've got rather a lot to tell you."

"What do you mean?" As Blake became alert his meek ness fell away from him and he was no longer just a mild little man with glasses and weary hair. He seemed, somehow, to get bigger.

"The man we're after, the go-between, he's connected in some way with the film unit."

"You're sure? How do you know?"

"Well," Paul gave a tired little sigh, "it's a long story. Look, can't you get away for a few minutes?"

"Not right now. I've got my own problems."

"What about Mandrake?"

"That's the problem. He's given me the slip."

"Oh." There didn't seem much else to say.

"It's nothing serious. At least, I don't think it is. I lost him a couple of days ago in Valencia. I believe he knows who I am, that's the main trouble. Otherwise it's not so bad. He's in Madrid now and I should know where to find him in the next couple of hours. But until I get that information I don't want to leave here."

"I see," Paul said. "Well, all right. I'll give you a ring, shall I?"

"Yes."

"One other thing," Paul said. "I want to hire a car." Now that he was on his own and Huxter had cut the umbilical cord that had attached him to the Peniscola hotel, a car was essential if he was to keep any sort of watch on the film people. And that, no matter how Blake might feel about it, was what he intended to do until he found out about those photographs.

"I'll fix that," Blake said. "If you're going to be helping me it's best to have a car that's not too easily traced—just in case something goes wrong. Look, ring me at four and we'll arrange a place to meet."

"Right. Till later then."

Across the street, the café customers were still drinking, still talking, lounging around unhurried and unworried as if they had nothing to do and a hell of a lot of time to do it in.

It was a great life, Paul thought. For some people.

CHAPTER SEVENTEEN

THE LOOTER

H E found a room in a small pension overlooking the Puerta de Alcala, the arch that was once part of the city walls, and slept until nearly four.

There was no phone in the place and he had to go down to the post office to call Blake. The telephone at the other end rang for some time and then Blake's voice said: "Hello. Blake here."

"Mr. Arthur sends his regards."

"Never mind that. Where are you?"

"What do you mean—never mind that?" Paul said. "I had strict instructions …"

"Yes, well we can forget about them. Where are you?"

"Well, never mind that either." It was hot in the phone box and Paul was annoyed now with Blake, irritated by the man's peremptory tone and nervous, edgy voice. "What about the car?"

There was a pause. When Blake spoke again his voice had changed. It was empty now. Nothing in it at all. "I'll leave it in a street near Retiro Park. It's better like that. If there's any kind of hitch it won't be associated with me. The keys will be in the dashboard and the door will be unlocked. I want you to pick it up no later than seven-fifteen tonight. Have you got that? It's better not to let it stand around too long."

"All right. How do I find it?"

"Take the Barcelona road and turn down the Avenue Menendez Pelayo. You'll see a large pink building. Go left past there and the car will be about a hundred yards down on the left hand side. It's a grey Seat. Not later than seven-fifteen, remember."

"Yes," Paul grunted, impatiently. "I know. When can we meet?"

"When you've got the car I'll be in the foyer at the Castellana Hilton." Again there was a pause. Blake said: "Where are you staying?"

"I can't remember." He couldn't either, not having taken any note of the pension's address. "I can find the place all right. I just can't remember what the street's called."

A large, slightly fearsome woman was pacing up and down outside the phone box making impatient gestures and glaring at Paul.

Blake said: "Look, are you sure you can't …"

"Quite sure. I'll have to go now. See you later."

He put the phone down and went back to his room. This time he took a careful note of the address.

It was one of those nights. First he had trouble finding a cab and when he did they were caught up in a traffic jam and it was nearly seven-thirty when the taxi turned into the Avenue Menendez Pelayo.

Fifteen minutes late. Paul hoped somebody hadn't pinched the car or something.

Just before the pink building they were snarled up again and he got out to walk the last few hundred yards. It was better, anyhow. A man arriving by cab to collect his car might, just, strike some onlooker as a little odd and there was no point in courting attention.

The grey Seat was still there, parked just where Blake had said it would be. Paul saw it as he rounded the corner and, relieved, stopped to light a cigarette. From somewhere nearby a church clock struck the half hour.

And at that second the grey car blew up.

One moment it stood there beside the kerb, a sleeping hunk of machinery. Then … a violent explosion, a gust of flame, a jet of smoke, chunks of flying metal. If anyone had been inside, he would now be scattered glutinously around the street.

Even fifty yards away the effect was stunning. Paul sprawled on hands and knees, watching in disbelief as the smoke cleared.

Suddenly the street was full of people—yelling, shouting people. Somebody started screaming for the police.

In the confusion, Paul picked himself up and slipped away, the absurdly obvious thought that "something's gone wrong" running round in his mind.

He had to get to Blake—fast. For the little details of the afternoon's phone conversation had assumed enormous significance. The insistence on his picking up the car at seven-fifteen. The pauses. The tension in Blake's voice. It was easy to guess now that somebody else had been with Blake that afternoon, somebody who had told him what to say and was in a position to make sure he said it. Somebody who had intended Paul to be in that car when the bomb went off.

If only he'd listened, really listened. For the warning had been there, he saw that now. Blake's refusal to go through the sacred identification ritual—that had been the clue. And Paul had missed it, ignored it.

Bitterly, cursing himself, he struggled through the crowd and found an empty taxi.

"What has happened, senor?" the driver asked.

"Nothing. A car caught fire, that's all. Nobody hurt." Thank God. He realised suddenly that his shirt was wet with a cold, clammy perspiration.

As usual he paid off the cab in the Gran Via and walked from there. Blake's shop was locked and there was a closed sign on the door. He thought about knocking; decided against it.

Nearby an alley led down to the back of the shops and Paul followed it to the yard behind Blake's premises. The gate in the wall was open and he went through it and approached the back door. That was locked, too, but beside it there was a window, big enough to climb through.

Paul looked around. Nobody was about.

He wrapped the butt of his automatic in his handkerchief and hit the window glass. It cracked and came away with a gentle, tinkling sound. He lifted the catch, opened the window and went in.

The room he found himself in was a parlour in the living quarters behind the shop. Nicely furnished. Scattered with the knick-knacks a man collects to remind himself of his travels.

No sound came from anywhere.

Paul tiptoed to the door, opened it, looked out into a passage. It was very dark and it took him some time to get his eyes accustomed to the gloom. When he had done so, he saw some stairs leading, presumably, to the bedrooms and opposite the stairs, another door, slightly ajar.

He crossed the passage and went in. The room turned out to be a study, very small, with a leather-topped desk and a couple of arm-chairs; a table with a long, slender lamp; a plum-coloured carpet; a wall of bookshelves. The curtains were drawn tight and little light filtered through.

Blake was lying on the floor, face downwards, the back of his coat soaked with a spreading stain of blood.

Paul knelt beside him and the man stirred and turned his face, a face so battered that it brought tremors of nausea to Paul's stomach.

"Lie still," Paul said. "I'll get help."

Blake tried to sit up, tried to speak. His eyes focused and shone briefly with recognition.

"You bastard," he said. "You stupid bastard." And then he died.

For a moment Paul stayed there, kneeling beside him. He felt guilty and wretched and he wanted to cry. He'd done everything wrong, right from the start. But nothing as bad as this. This was the worst. If only he'd listened. If only he'd thought. There might have been—must have been—something he could have done.

After a while he stood up, heavily, and looked around. The room had been searched, neatly and systematically. Papers from the desk had been taken out, examined and stacked in piles against the wall. The bindings of the books had been cut open. If the room had ever held any secrets it was a safe bet that it held none now.

The same, inevitably, would be true of the rest of the building. Whoever had gone through this room had known what he was about. There'd be no clues here or anywhere else for anyone.

Paul turned back towards Blake's body—and froze, like a child playing statues.

Upstairs a floorboard had creaked and now, as he listened, he could hear footsteps, soft but not particularly stealthy, as if whoever it was believed himself to be alone in the place, coming down the stairs.

Paul dropped to one knee and drew his automatic.

The steps came closer. In the passage now. Closer. Closer.

With dramatic suddenness the figure of a man was silhouetted in the doorway.

Paul yelled: "Hold it. Right there ..."

The man whirled, his arm went back and something glinted in his hand. Impulsively, not thinking, Paul squeezed the trigger. The sound of the shot bounced back deafeningly from the walls, faded, and roared up again as the man's hand came forward and Paul fired a second time.

Smoke and the smell of cordite filled the room.

The man in the doorway pressed his hands to his stomach. The knife he had been holding dropped softly to the carpet. His knees bent and he fell, gracefully, in slow motion, to the floor and lay quite still.

Paul let him lie there, his revolver aimed at the dark head, until he was sure the man would never move again. Then he went across and heaved him over on to his back.

The dead eyes of Josef stared up at him, fixed eternally on a point immeasurably far away and a little to the right of Paul's head.

In his turn, Paul looked down at the crumpled body, the empty envelope which, only a minute ago, had been a quick and intelligent, even likeable, man.

It was the first time he had killed anyone and he wasn't enjoying it. The fact that Josef had, almost certainly, been involved in the attempt to kill him and in the murder of Blake hardly seemed to matter. Such thoughts were no defence against the horror and remorse that Paul felt.

What he wanted to do was to run like hell away from this place, and yet he couldn't. For what he had to do was to search the body and the very thought of it was nauseating. From being a man with a mind and a soul, Josef had been transformed into a carcass and the fact that Paul himself had been the butcher made things no easier.

Gently, he rolled the body over until it lay face down again and he no longer had to look into the eyes and then, almost with reverence, he began to empty the pockets.

The contents of the coat revealed at once what Josef had been doing there. Looting. There was a wad of pesetas, a gold cigarette lighter, a Shaeffer pen, a gold Longines watch. And a wedding ring.

Paul went back to Blake's body. On the third finger of the left hand there was a pale circle where the ring used to nestle. It had never occurred to Paul that Blake might have been married and the discovery saddened him. He put the ring back on the finger and returned to Josef.

There was little more to find. No papers, no documents except the kind a man normally carried. Paul left all the stuff on the floor and sat down wearily in the chair by the desk to review the situation.

There must have been two men here at least for Josef alone could hardly have forced Blake to set the trap with the car.

He remembered, suddenly, Blake's insistence on knowing where he was staying and thanked God that he had been unable to remember. With that information, Josef's friends would not have had to rely on his being in the car when the bomb exploded. They could have picked him off any time.

Josef, though. Where did he fit into the pattern? He could have been, probably was, the slighter of the two hooded men in the bodega. Small-time, anyway … a thief who had come back after Blake had been killed to strip the body and the house of anything of value.

He had been greedy and greed had cost him his life. Paul's remorse eased a little.

He got up and looked over the rest of the building. Every room had been searched as thoroughly as the study. All he found was a few personal letters and photographs, among them a snapshot of a gravestone with an inscription that read: 'In loving memory of Mary Kate Blake, 1905-1959.' A picture of a rather plain woman, signed 'All my love, darling, always—Mary' stood, framed, on Blake's bedside table.

Paul went downstairs. There was nothing here for him.

In the shop itself, though, there was something. Blake's assistant lay on the floor behind the counter. He had been shot in the chest and, by the look of him, had been dead for several hours.

His sensitivity about handling corpses now slightly blunted by practice, Paul searched him and Blake, too. Again nothing.

He took a last look round and let himself out by the back door.

It was nine o'clock. The heat of the day had gone and the night was no more than pleasantly warm. All around, the bars and restaurants were coming to life as people emerged from their homes in search of food and drink and entertainment.

Paul went back to his room, washed and went out again. He killed an hour sitting at a sidewalk café with a carafe of wine and at some stage he forced himself to eat.

Then he sat for a while, smoking a cigarette and watching the girls go by. He wondered what Emma would be doing; who she would be with. Not that it could matter any more. Whatever she may once have thought of him, her feelings would hardly be very warm now.

He stubbed out his cigarette in his wine glass and watched with moody satisfaction as the paper came apart and sodden tobacco floated disgustingly on the cold, pale surface.

He thought of Huxter and Grainger and all the others who made up that curious little group in the Peniscola Hotel.

One of them, he was sure, was a killer, a spy of sorts. Maybe more than one of them. But who?

Thinking led him gently round in circles and brought him remorselessly back to where he started. All he knew for sure was that Josef had been involved somehow in the business that had brought him to Spain. Yet Josef could hardly have been the go-between. That role must have been played by someone else, someone free to travel frequently between London and Madrid. Someone like … like any of those others.

And then there was Mandrake. Last but most important of all. Where the hell was he?

The clock on the restaurant wall showed 11.20. Paul paid his bill and left, strolling slowly, blending perfectly with the crowd of evening pleasure-seekers. He had plenty of time.

CHAPTER EIGHTEEN

RAPE! RAPE!

J UST before midnight he got to the Peniscola Hotel and stood for a few minutes on the other side of the road, smoking a cigarette and watching, without much curiosity, the comings and goings of the guests.

He waited till he heard a clock strike twelve and then he walked to the back of the building and climbed the fire escape.

On this side of the hotel a ledge about six inches wide ran underneath the windows and terminated at the double balcony outside the corner suite which, on the second floor, was occupied by the Huxters.

Paul took a deep breath and stepped out onto the ledge. For a few seconds he concentrated simply on staying there, plastered against the wall, while he fought down the tight feeling of fear and giddiness in his head.

Then, slowly, sweating, he edged his way along. Just his luck that the room he wanted should have been on this side. Had it been around the corner, where his own room was, he could have got there by the much simpler method of leaping from balcony to balcony.

Somebody ought to complain, he thought crazily. There should be balconies outside every room. Call itself a first-class hotel? Rubbish. Nobody should be put to this inconvenience.

By the time he reached his objective he was a little light-headed. A metal band seemed to have been strung round his temples and slowly pulled tight and for the last few yards he fought a compulsive urge to step backwards and let himself fall the two storeys to the ground. The death wish. That was all he needed.

To his relief the window he sought was open and he let himself in. He was trembling a little.

He drew the curtains and switched on the bedside lamp. Everything was neat and clean. The furnishings were sparse—a single bed, a chest of drawers, a table and a chair—but well polished and tidy.

Josef had been a fastidious man.

Beside the bed was a panel with room numbers in measured columns and above each number a small bulb that lit up when someone in one of the rooms pressed the button for Josef. Right now all the bulbs were dark.

Paul went first to the chest and examined the contents of the top drawer. Shirts and handkerchiefs, underwear, a bundle of love letters. He put everything back and opened the second drawer.

Behind him there was the soft burr of a buzzer and one of the bulbs on the panel glared out like a bloodshot eye. Paul stood quite still, waiting. After a moment the buzzing stopped and the light went out. He unfroze and went on with his search.

The second drawer, too, contained only personal things and he was about to begin on the third when the buzzer started again. More persistent this time, a continuous, impatient sound. The red eye looked furious.

Paul watched it for a while, then shrugged. In a minute whoever wanted Josef would come to the conclusion that the man was off-duty and give up.

He opened the third drawer—and struck gold. Literally. It was full of expensive cigarette cases, lighters, powder compacts, wrist watches.

Josef, calm, efficient, obliging Josef, had been a thief, tending the needs of his guests with one hand and robbing them blind with the other. It was an unexpected facet of his personality but one which, at least, tallied with his return visit to Blake's boutique that evening.

Gold and silver twinkled like the lights on a Christmas tree as Paul scrabbled through the loot but the drawer held nothing else of any interest and he was about to close it when the door of the room started to open, cautiously, as if the intruder was not entirely sure that the room was empty.

Swiftly Paul put out the light and dropped down beside the bed, his gun in his hand, his heart yo-yoing about in his chest.

The door creaked gently. Light crept in from the corridor. A cough—hesitant, soft. A pause. The door closed. The overhead light went on.

Emma Dane was standing there with a key in her hand.

"Don't make a sound," Paul murmured. "I'd hate to have to shoot you." He was on his knees, the automatic aimed at her left nipple, or—since she was decently clad—where her left nipple might reasonably have been expected to be.

She stared at him; tried to speak but the words ran into each other, making a low, bleating sound in her throat.

"What are you doing here?" he said.

Composure returned to her with a speed which he found quite admirable. She sat down on the wooden chair beside the table and fixed him with cold, blue eyes. Her white, severely simple cocktail dress, was snug and just revealing enough to put erotic thoughts into Paul's mind. This was never particularly difficult but the rounded, tanned skin that showed above the neckline instilled even more erotic thoughts than usual. He found himself licking his lips and stopped it at once.

"I don't see why I should answer your questions," she said. finally.

"Well …" He sounded almost apologetic. "I do have a gun, you know."

She nodded. "I doubt if you'd use it. Do put it away."

"You won't scream?"

"Don't be absurd."

He put the gun back in its shoulder holster and had the satisfaction of seeing her eyes widen a little at this apparently professional touch. "All right," he said. "Now what are you doing here?"

She let the key fall from her hand onto the bed. "To return that. It's Josef's master key. He must have left it in my room when he was tidying up this evening and I found it when I got back after dinner. I kept ringing the bell but he didn't come, so I thought I'd bring it to his room and leave it. That's what I was doing when you came leaping out, armed to the teeth."

"I see." It sounded plausible enough. It might even be true.

She reached into her black, suede evening bag and brought out a cigarette. "By the way," she said. "Where *is* Josef?"

Paul hesitated. Almost without realising he was going to say it, "He's dead," he said.

"What! I don't believe you."

"It's true. He was shot."

"When—today?"

"Yes." He hardly knew why he had told her all this and yet he was glad he had. There came a point, even in a job like his, where you had to trust someone, if only a little, and he would rather trust her than anyone else, even though he might be making the biggest mistake of them all.

"But … who killed him? Why?"

"I ..." Trust had its limit and this was it. "I can't tell you any more."

"You keep *saying* that," she said, irritably. "It's really very frustrating."

"I'm sorry. There's nothing I can do about it."

"Your lips are sealed, no doubt." There was an ironic gleam in her eyes. He ignored it.

"I'll tell you one thing," he said, "Josef was a right villain." He showed her the collection of trinkets in the drawer.

"Good God," she said. "Old ever-faithful Josef. Who'd have dreamed ..."

"Look. Will you promise to sit there quietly till I've finished looking around?"

"What will you do if I refuse?"

He sighed, helplessly. "I don't know."

"I promise. Anyway, I'm as curious as you are." She sat quietly, smoking, while he searched the room, finding nothing until he looked in the most obvious place of all—under the bed. What he discovered there was a small, tin box. With a satisfied grunt he pulled it out and put it on the bed to open it.

She came and stood beside him as he lifted the lid.

Inside were four copies of the photograph that she and the Lady Wife had received that morning. And beneath them was the negative.

Emma drew breath sharply as she looked again at the obscene pictures. "What ... what does this mean?"

"It means," said Paul, "that Josef sent those photographs to you and Huxter's wife. It also means, probably, that he took them."

"And you were telling the truth—they *were* faked?"

He glanced at her. "What do you think?" With something like gladness in her voice, she said: "It does look like it, doesn't it?" And then she said: "But why?"

"It's a long story." He was standing at the door, listening, only half-attending to Emma now.

In the passage there was the sound of people drifting up to bed.

Paul opened the door and peeped out. Nobody was in sight, although round the bend he could hear voices going away into the distance.

"Out you go," he said. "And, remember, don't tell anyone about any of this."

"Cross my heart." She crossed it, making the childish gesture oddly suggestive.

"Good." Impulsively, he leaned over and kissed her on the lips. "Sleep well."

She stopped just for a second at the door. "Will I see you again?"

"I don't know. There are certain things I have to clear up. But I'm going to need an outsize piece of luck."

"I hope you get it." Then she was gone, leaving behind her, like a sexy Cheshire cat, the memory of a last, warm smile.

Paul tidied the room, pocketed the photographs and the negative and went back to the window. The prospect of crawling along that ledge again seemed extremely unattractive, the drop to the ground neck-breakingly far.

The window he had used the previous night, the one that gave onto the fire escape was a much pleasanter proposition. He went back to the door, listened, and let himself out.

He had gone about five paces when he heard the voices of two men approaching around the bend. Masters and Breugelhoffer.

Paul scampered back to Josef's room. The door was shut—and he had left the key inside.

Panicking, he grabbed the handle of the door to the adjacent room, turned it and—"Thank God," he breathed—it was unlocked. He slipped inside, closed the door and kept still. The room was in darkness. Nothing moved. Nobody screamed.

In the passage footsteps approached; stopped. The sound of conversation droned softly.

"Damn," Paul said. Now it was that bloody ledge or nothing. He moved into the room, groping towards the window.

He was halfway there when a voice from one of the twin beds said: "Who's that?"

And now he realised the true horror of the situation. He had stumbled into the Huxters' suite—and the Lady Wife was in bed. He stood where he was, shocked and dumb.

"Come on," she said. "Who the hell's that?"

Paul looked at the door, then at the window. No good. He was trapped. She would be up and yelling before he could reach either exit.

"It's me," he said, his voice hoarse.

His eyes now accustomed to the dark, he could just see her, a vague outline against the bedhead. By the same token, she could see him.

"God Almighty!" she said. "You've got a nerve. Get out of here!"

"All right. If that's how you feel ..." He went to the door. Masters and Breugelhoffer were still talking. Now what? If he could only keep her quiet until they had gone ...

"Listen," he said. "The way I've behaved to you ... I'm I'm deeply sorry about it ... I've been thinking about you and ..."

"Crap," she said, harshly. "You're a liar. Now get out."

Paul straightened up. The conversation outside had stopped. "Okay," he said. "I won't force myself on you ..."

Then ... "No wait ... Come here." Her tone had grown softer, full of invitation.

He paused, turned, curious about this sudden change of mind.

She was sitting up against the pillows and at close range her impressive breasts were clearly visible beneath the thin stuff of her nightgown.

"Come on," she whispered. With remarkable speed her left arm snaked out, twined itself around his neck and pulled his head down until his nose was poised just above her cleavage. Crashing waves of Je Reviens burst upon him. "What are you waiting for?"

"Nothing. I …" Paul struggled to keep his face from being enveloped in all that quivering softness and wondered, frantically, what to do next.

"I've thought a lot about you, too," she said.

Behind him Paul heard a footstep, soft, cautious. He wrenched himself away from her, understanding now why her mood had changed so dramatically.

A man, a man who must have been concealed in the bathroom all the time, had opened the door and was letting himself stealthily out into the corridor.

And that man was Larry Grainger.

Paul rushed after him but by the time he had disengaged himself from the Lady Wife's clutching fingers and made it to the door, Grainger had vanished—and J. J. Huxter was getting out of the lift and heading towards the conjugal pleasures of his bedroom.

At the same time the Lady Wife was raising hell. "Help! Police! Oh, help me! Rape!"

Huxter stopped dead. The cigar fell, as if smitten, from his lips and he came bounding down the corridor like a fat but faithful old dog whose mistress was in distress.

Paul slammed the door, locked it and raced back across the bedroom. Ledge, here I come!

The Lady Wife was standing on the bed, her nightdress gathered round her, her face scarlet as she gathered breath for another onslaught on the night air. Paul grabbed up a cushion and hurled it at her as he passed.

"Ah, shut up!" Then he was at the window, through it and on the balcony. Of course! There was no ledge. Alone of all the rooms on that side of the hotel, this one had a balcony.

Behind him Huxter was trying to open the door, the Lady Wife was screaming, the corridor was filling with people.

There was only one thing for it. He went to the edge of the balcony, clambered onto the wall and prepared to drop to the ground, thirty feet below.

Just for once, Fate chose to be kind. The restaurant roof jutted out ten feet beneath the Huxters' room and Paul landed on it on hands and knees, with a jolt that left him breathless.

He lay still for a moment or two then, inspired purely by panic, he swung himself, Tarzan-style, towards a tree that loomed up in the garden a few yards away. His fingers caught and held a jutting branch and, with an agility that astonished him, he climbed on it and along it until he was crouched against the trunk, hidden by the foliage. He stayed there, panting.

In every room on that side of the hotel, lights came on. People leaned out of their windows, calling to each other for information.

Hotel staff broke out like a pink rash on the lawns. Voices Spanish and English, swirled around him as he clung to the safety of his tree.

He could hear a dozen people asking: "What happened? Who was it? What did he do? Where did he go?"

He could hear someone saying: "Where is Josef?"

And he could hear Huxter yelling: "Screw Josef! Where's the bastard who raped my wife?"

Down below torches tore the darkness to shreds. Somebody mentioned the police. Somebody else called for a shotgun. Someone, brighter than the rest, began to shine his torch upwards, into the trees.

Paul gave himself up for lost.

And then, timely as the arrival on the cinema screen of the United States Cavalry, relief came. There was a sudden cry of "There he goes!" and in minutes the garden was empty as the searchers left off searching and set out in pursuit of a lone, terror-stricken pedestrian who, seeing them coming, began yelling hoarsely and running for the sanctuary of the bright lights in the city centre.

When everyone had gone and the heads had vanished from the windows, Paul climbed down from the tree.

Half an hour later he was back in his own room.

CHAPTER NINETEEN

AN OUTSIZE PIECE OF LUCK

S OON after noon the next day he was sitting in a car outside the Peniscola Hotel, waiting. What he was waiting for, he was not entirely certain. But Larry Grainger figured in it somewhere. After last night and the night before, Grainger had some explaining to do.

Paul had been up early that morning. He had breakfasted in his room and then gone out to hire a car. He had hired it, as a precaution, under an assumed name and since he had no papers in that name it had cost him plenty.

Now he sat and watched and smoked. He wasn't feeling happy. Without Blake, without easy access to the Peniscola and its inhabitants, he was a blind man without a stick, working on instinct and trusting to Providence to show him the way.

The morning papers had made no mention of the murder of Blake and the other two men and that had been worrying. Paul had hoped the bodies would be found quickly, the British Embassy notified and the information passed, through official channels, to Mr. Chatham and the Department.

Now it seemed it was up to him to break the news. He thought of going to the Embassy and asking their help but he could hardly do that without seriously implicating himself. The only other line of action was to phone Mr. Chatham personally and this he did.

He made the call from a café and waited, drinking coffee, until it came through. He waited two hours.

Then Mr. Chatham was on the line and when Paul had gone through the identification ritual he said: "It's about Blake …"

"I've heard," Mr. Chatham said grimly. "The police found the bodies this morning. The Embassy called me ten minutes ago."

"You'd better know this," Paul said. "I killed the third man myself."

"What third man? There were only two bodies—Blake and his shop assistant."

Then what had happened to Josef? Had his associates missed him, traced him back to Blake's shop and removed his body? If this were so, and it was at least plausible, it indicated that the people connected with Josef were also connected with the Peniscola Hotel and were anxious not to involve it in a police investigation. If nothing else, it was another piece of evidence, flimsy perhaps, linking Huxter's film unit with Mandrake.

He explained this as simply as he could to Mr. Chatham.

"I see." Mr. Chatham said. "Did Blake tell you where Mandrake was?"

"No. I thought he'd told you."

"Well, he didn't. We didn't hear from him at all yesterday."

"Oh, Lord. What do you want me to do now?"

"Nothing. Just wait. I'm sending two men to Madrid at once. Conway and Allen—you remember them, I believe. They were the ones who brought you in to see me. They'll be in Madrid, at the Felix Hotel, by five this evening. Contact them there, tell them everything that's happened and, if you would, place yourself at their disposal."

"Right."

Mr. Chatham hesitated. "I'm sorry to have involved you in this, Baker. Until the last day or so we had everything under control. Now it's all gone wildly wrong."

"Well, if I can help …"

"Just contact Conway and Allen, that's all."

After the phone call Paul drove across to the Peniscola and parked. It was a token gesture, really. Beyond questioning Grainger he had little idea of what he could do. But he felt he ought to do something, since time surely must be running out.

But, again, what? How could he help? If Mandrake's deal had not already been completed it must certainly be done soon and Paul, alone, seemed powerless to stop it. Well, it wasn't his fault. He had blundered, of course. No point in denying that.

But didn't the blame lie with the Department, with Mr Chatham? He had underestimated the significance of that publicity hand-out, had thought it too remote to be important. Well, that was *his* mistake. He had sent a boy when he should have sent a man, an amateur when he should have sent a professional.

The murder of Rosemary was also mentioned in the morning papers but briefly and with little emphasis. The police, apparently, were working on the assumption that she had been killed by a maniac and nobody seemed to regard the matter as being of any great moment. Prostitutes had always been fair game for sex maniacs and the likelihood of a violent death was one of the hazards of the occupation.

Paul lit his fourth cigarette in an hour and wiped his face with a handkerchief. It was going to be one hell of a warm day.

At 12.30, the great glass doors of the Peniscola were flung ceremoniously open and Larry Grainger came out. At the bottom of the steps he turned left and went into the bar-tobacconist next to the hotel.

Paul got out of the car, crossed the road and waited in the narrow passage that led to the hotel gardens.

He had not long to wait. Grainger left the tobacconist and headed towards the taxi rank at the corner. As he passed the alley, Paul grabbed his arm and yanked him in. It was quickly done—a now-you-see-it, now-you-don't sleight of hand.

Nobody could have seen it happen.

Grainger was spread-eagled against the wall, staring at Paul with panic in his eyes.

"Wha … what the hell's going on?"

"I want to talk to you," Paul said.

Grainger tried to push him away. "Well, for Christ's sake, there's no need to get rough. I haven't done anything."

"No? That's what I want to find out." Paul was leaning on him, his left hand pressing firmly against Grainger's chest, his right free and poised to strike should the necessity arise.

Grainger said: "Well, get off me, can't you? I can hardly breathe with you leaning all over me."

Paul eased off a little, still watching him warily. "Where-ever I go, you seem to be there, too. You were in La Nottee, the night before last. You were in Huxter's room last night. It all seems rather curious—as if you were following me around."

"Following you around?" Grainger sounded bitter. "The other way about, if you ask me. Everywhere I go, you turn up and queer my pitch. Ever since I got to this bloody town, you've ruined every chance I've had of getting laid. I was doing all right with Emma until you put the mockers on it. Okay, you want to know what I was doing at La Nottee? Looking for a bird, that's what. What else was anyone doing there?"

He lit one of the cigarettes he had just bought and scowled at Paul resentfully. "And then last night," he went on, "that was the crowning touch all right. I'd been trying to get the Huxter woman into bed for days and then, just as I was there, practically on the agony stroke, you come bursting into the room to rape her." He threw the spent match away. "What were you doing there, anyway? I thought you'd been drummed out of Madrid."

"I decided not to go." Paul was faintly bewildered. He had not expected Grainger to react at all in this aggrieved way.

"Old J.J.'s livid with you," Grainger said, eyes glinting with satisfaction. "He called the police out last night. Says you assaulted his old woman."

"Does he? I suppose he knows you were there, too."

Grainger's smile vanished to be replaced by an expression of acute anxiety. "No. He doesn't, as a matter of fact."

"Well, if you tell anyone you've seen me today, he bloody soon will. We can share the same prison cell, you and I. That'll be cosy." Paul dropped into a thoughtful silence and Grainger asked: "Can I go now?"

"No. Listen, that night I got so drunk in La Nottee—were you there?"

"Yes. Practically everyone was. Why?"

"Did you come into the bedroom when I was with that woman, Rosemary?"

"No, certainly not." Grainger was indignant. "What do you think I am, a bloody *voyeur*?"

"Then you didn't see who took those pictures of me and the girl?"

"No, how could I? Look, what *is* this all about? You don't seem to realise it but you're in a lot of trouble and ..."

"Shut up. Someone's coming."

Footsteps approached the entrance to the alley and in a moment a man went by. A man in a green hat and a blue jacket and large round sunglasses.

"Blimey," Grainger said. "Look at old Miguel."

Miguel ... the man of leisure who had been sitting at the café opposite Blake's boutique that first day. The man Paul had envied for having nothing to do but sit there with a newspaper and a drink. That had been Miguel.

And Paul had been so careful to ensure that nobody followed him. That was the funny bit. Of course nobody had followed him. There had been no need to.

The people who employed Josef and Miguel knew who Blake was. They knew an agent was coming from London. They knew that agent would contact Blake. So all they had to do was have someone, Miguel, watching the boutique to see who turned up. And Paul had just barged in without a thought for security, confident in his ignorance and lack of experience, that he alone knew of Blake's dual profession.

That was the mistake he had made, the first, blundering, simple error that the man in the bodega had mentioned. By going to Blake's place like that he had advertised his identity as clearly as if he had gone around handing out business cards inscribed 'Paul Baker. Secret Agent. Licensed to kill with gun, knife or bare hands.'

"You bloody fool," he said to himself.

And to Grainger he said: "Go on, beat it. And remember— keep your mouth shut."

By the time Grainger had gone, Miguel was in the parking lot, climbing astride a motor-cycle. His green hat had been replaced by a black crash helmet. He kicked the bike into life and drove slowly away towards the centre of town.

Paul got into his car and followed, staying about fifty yards behind as the motor-cycle turned left past the post office, through the arch that provided the view from Paul's room, and out of town. The job was easy, for Miguel had no idea he was being tailed.

Paul sucked at an unlit cigarette and coasted along, keeping his eyes on the black crash helmet.

For the moment he had lost interest in Grainger. The man had shown resentment where Paul had expected guilt or even fear. He had acted, indeed, like a man innocent of everything except perhaps an over-zealous desire to seduce his host's wife. Well, good luck to you, Paul thought, remembering the venom of which the Lady Wife was capable.

Miguel, though, was a different matter and one he blamed himself for not having considered earlier. From the start he had paid little attention to the man, just as he had to Josef, accepting them in the way you accept certain kinds of people—postmen, for instance, or shop assistants—who are where you expect to find them, doing what you expect them to do.

Another mistake that had been. After last night when Josef's interest in the affair had been revealed, Paul might, at least, have wondered a little about Miguel.

And yet … because the uncle was a villain, did it necessarily follow that the nephew was one, too?

The motor-cycle did a steady thirty miles an hour along the Barcelona Road. Paul looked out at scenery that was becoming familiar, scenery that he had passed two days before on his way to the film location. Perhaps that was where Miguel was heading, engaged in nothing more sinister than delivering a message to someone on the unit.

Just his luck, Paul thought, if this turned out to be a colossal waste of time. Still, having committed himself this far, he carried on and received his reward when Miguel continued past the turn-off to the location.

Paul looked at his watch. So far he had been driving for a little over an hour.

When he looked up again, Miguel had disappeared.

Paul had rounded a sharpish bend less than a minute behind the motor-cycle and now the road stretched straight and empty for a mile ahead. It was unlikely that Miguel could have covered that distance in so short a time. So he must have turned off. But where?

Paul did a swift U-turn and went back the way he had come, examining the other side of the road for a concealed turning. Just before he reached the bend again he found one—a gateway, set back from the verge and difficult to spot unless you were actually looking for it.

He parked off the road and walked back to the gate. Only the chirping of the birds and the distant grumble of traffic disturbed the stillness as he crept cautiously to the opening and peered through.

Almost without being aware of it, he had his automatic in his hand.

The gate opened onto a narrow, pebbled drive that wound through shrubbery and trees to a villa, barely visible from where Paul stood, about a quarter of a mile from the road.

He vaulted over the gate and plunged into the shrubbery, using it as cover as he followed the lines of the drive.

The dryness of his throat, the over-rapid beat of his heart, the slight tremble in his limbs—all the sensations of excitement and danger which had become so familiar to him lately were back again. He put the safety catch on the gun in case he should inadvertently pull the trigger as he stumbled through the undergrowth.

The shrubbery ended abruptly and Paul found himself crouched on the edge of a lawn some thirty yards from the front of the villa. Miguel's motor-cycle was parked near the door and a tall man whom Paul had never seen before was leaning against the wall, his hat tipped over his eyes. The bulge of a shoulder holster was clearly visible through his tight linen jacket.

Paul edged his way round, protected by the shrubs, until he was at the back of the building. Between him and it were two small outhouses, garden sheds, that offered a sort of cover for the dash across the open expanse of lawn.

Behind him the shrubbery thinned away till it terminated in a rough paddock that led, in turn, to a high fence. Beyond that fence, half a mile away, he could see the bulk of the empty palace where Huxter's unit was filming.

He took a deep breath, clenched his fist tightly around the pistol, slipped off the safety catch and scampered wildly towards the first shed. Sweat streamed from his face and body, every nerve in him stretched to snapping point and at each hectic stride he expected to hear, at best, a shout of alarm, at worst the angry crack of a gun. He heard neither.

Flat against the wooden wall of one shed, he prepared himself for the dash to the second. He dashed. Again nobody challenged him and now he was only ten yards from the villa itself.

Everything was silent. Curtained windows stared back at him, empty as the half-closed eyes of a corpse.

Another frantic scuttle and he was hugging the brickwork of the main building. It loomed over him, white walled and green-tiled, a combination that explained why it was so hard to see from the road.

From beyond the corner came the murmur of voices and in a moment, treading lightly, he sidled along the wall and looked round.

A few yards away, double french doors stood open and steps led down from them to a small terrace where a table was set for lunch. There were places for two people.

From the room beyond the french doors came the sound of voices.

Paul edged closer, taking it slowly and softly. A large water barrel with some kind of flowering shrub in it stood beside the window and Paul crouched down behind it. By easing himself a little to the left he could see into the room, a room filled with the nondescript bits and pieces that people throw together when they let a place furnished. Drab armchairs, a table or two, an ugly, ornate wall cabinet, a rather worn rug. The ubiquitous Tretchikoff orchid was framed on one wall.

All these things he noticed with his first quick glance and with his second he saw Miguel.

The man was standing beside a table, a glass of beer in one hand, his crash helmet tucked under his arm. His attitude was one of respect, almost that of a man standing at attention.

Beside him, in an arm-chair, looking bored and petulant, was a small, slim, long-haired youth in a blush pink shirt and pale blue hipster slacks. The ends of the shirt were knotted around his stomach, showing a narrow expanse of tanned, hairless skin. He had a chunky gold identity bracelet around one wrist and a medallion hung from a gold chain around his neck. His feet were bare.

A lock of black hair flopped with cultivated carelessness down his forehead and curled away above his right eyebrow. Against the swarthy, smooth darkness of his face, his mouth was a soft bow, crimson as a lipstick advert.

Miguel was saying: "Very well, senor. What shall I tell them?"

He was talking not to the youth but to a third man, who was sitting just out of Paul's view across the room.

Paul snaked a little further round the barrel to look at this other man, although he had no need to. He knew who it was, who it had to be. Henry Mandrake was sprawled on a settee, relaxed and at his ease.

He was about medium height and plump, like a middle-aged cherub, rather than fat. His fair hair had thinned on top and now it was brushed carefully across in the forlorn hope that what remained would do the work of what had once been there.

He was deeply sunburned and his rather round blue eyes showed up startlingly bright against the golden tan surrounding them. Like the youth he wore a pink shirt and blue slacks and his feet were bare. The insteps and each toe bore individual clumps of thick, blond hair.

Paul examined him with care, noting the slightly fleshy nose, the rounded chin and the thin mouth that was unexpectedly hard against the softness of the rest of his face.

Long before he spoke Paul knew what his voice would sound like. It would sound like the voice in the bodega, the voice on the phone.

The voice he had heard a dozen times during Mandrake's political career, speaking on the radio, giving television interviews … the rich, smooth politician's voice, droning its message of good cheer to the electorate, heard but only casually listened to; the kind of voice which, heard again in some other place and some other context, was both familiar and not quite familiar.

Now it said: "Tell them to be here at eight o'clock with proof that the final payment has been made into my bank. The Zurich bank, remember. I'll have the film ready for them. Do you understand that?"

"Si, senor. Will you want me to come, too?"

Mandrake shook his head. "No. We won't need you any more."

"Si, senor. Is there anything else?"

"Yes. This man Baker. Have they found him yet?"

"No, senor. But the police are looking for him. It seems he tried to rape Mrs. Huxter last night."

Mandrake chuckled, not without admiration. "Really? What a lusty young man he is. Well, never mind. It doesn't really matter who gets him first—us or the police. Either way, I don't think he's dangerous. All right, Miguel, you can go."

Miguel hesitated, uncertain which exit to use. Finally he decided on the french windows. Paul cringed back against the wall. The moment when Miguel stopped on the threshold was agony to him. He raised his automatic and aimed it steadily waiting for the shout of alarm when his presence was discovered.

It did not come.

Instead, Miguel said: "Goodbye, Senor Mandrake. It has been a great honour to know you."

"Yes," Mandrake said, absently. "I expect it has."

Miguel carried on down the steps, crossed the terrace and vanished around the front of the villa. In a minute there came the sound of his motor-cycle starting up.

Paul stayed where he was and pondered his next move. There was something, he supposed, to be said for leaping into the room, gun in hand, and forcing Mandrake to give up the film he had mentioned, for it was obvious what that film contained.

But having done that …? There was still the problem of disposing of Mandrake and the long-haired boy, not to mention the armed guard outside. The thought of shooting them all on the spot was too bloodthirsty to contemplate.

Besides, even if he got hold of the film and somehow, short of murder, managed to get away, there remained still the question of the go-between. His identity hadn't been established yet.

Paul made up his mind. Surely the smart thing to do was to leave now, contact Conway and Allen and return with them this evening when the final swapping of money and microfilm was to take place. Yes, that would be best.

In the room, the silence which had followed Miguel's departure was broken. Mandrake stirred, sat up straight on the settee, held out his arms to the long-haired youth. "Come here, you," he said, softly.

Paul waited no longer. Feeling a little unclean, as if he had been caught peeping through a bedroom keyhole, he backed away and returned unobtrusively to the protection of the shrubbery.

Five minutes later he was in his car and on his way back to Madrid.

CHAPTER TWENTY

THE TIME FOR TRUST

On the outskirts of town he stopped and phoned Emma at the Peniscola Hotel.

"Paul! Where are you? I suppose you know the police are looking for you?"

"Yes," he said. "I heard."

"Oh. Well, you sound awfully calm about it."

He did. He was amazed how calm he sounded. He even felt calm. When you'd been beaten up and almost blown up, when you'd shot a man, when a woman had been stabbed to death beside you, when—at times—you'd seemed to be wading through a flowing sea of corpses, a little matter like being wanted by the police on a rape charge was of slight importance.

"Are they still at the hotel?" he asked.

"Oh, yes. They were asking questions all night and again this morning. There are hordes of them waiting about downstairs."

"Can you get out?"

"Well, yes and no. The bogeys have orders to keep an eye on anyone who knows you. In case one of us is still in touch with you, I suppose. Anyway, there's a dear little sad man in the lobby who tags along wherever I go. It's awfully pathetic. He's got such short legs and has to walk ever so fast to keep up."

"What about the back way?"

"The police are there, too."

"Pity. I was going to ask you to meet me for lunch but it seems a bit dangerous. Listen, what about Josef?"

"Oh, yes. Great excitement. The police are after him as well. They found all that stuff in his room. Not the pictures, though. I suppose you took them. Were they what you were after?"

"Sort of," Paul said, non-committally. "Look, I want you to do something for me. Can you find out who was responsible for having Josef and Miguel appointed just to look after us? Hotels don't usually do that sort of thing off their own bat. It would have to be by request. Can you manage that?"

"Easy," she said. "I'm having a drink with the assistant manager in a minute."

"Really?" The word came out sharper than he'd intended.

"Jealous?"

"Who? Me?"

"Beast!"

"I'll call you later. Will you be in your room about sevenish?"

"I'll make a point of it. I'll just be getting ready for my bath then. Stripped down to pants and suspender belt. Of course, we cater for all tastes here. If you prefer something a bit more kinky, like high leather boots and a nurse's cap, I'll see what I can do to oblige." Her voice was down to a sexy, exaggerated stage whisper which Paul found highly provocative.

"I can hardly wait," he said.

"Good."

He moved the conversation back to less erotic grounds. "I suppose the police have a description of me?"

"Oh, yes. I helped them with it."

"Thanks very much."

"Well, what else could I do? There wasn't much point in giving them wrong information. They'd only have got suspicious. Anyway, they think you're about two metres tall—are you?"

"Roughly."

"Really?" She sounded doubtful. "Metres make you sound awfully big, don't they? Still, that's what they worked it out at. And dark hair and blue eyes. Last seen wearing a black sports coat and grey slacks."

He made a note to do something about changing those details a little. Then he said: "Is Miguel at the hotel now?"

"No. It's his day off. He won't be in till tomorrow."

"Good. I'll call you at seven, then."

"Okay." She paused. Then she asked: "Did you really try to rape Mrs. Huxter?"

"Are you mad? You don't know what that woman's like. She's a killer. She …"

"*You* seem to know rather a lot about her." She was all icy again.

"Observation," he said. "Just observation. Believe me, I'd rather rape Huxter than her."

"You don't seem to like her much."

"No, I don't."

She gave a smug little laugh. "Good. Well, 'bye then."

They hung up. It seemed to Paul that for someone he was not entirely sure he could trust he was putting an awful lot of faith in Emma. Well, the hell with it. The business was nearly over now. Conway and Allen—he had a fleeting, absurd vision of them in shaggy coats and battered hats singing 'Underneath the Arches'—would be here soon to finish things. And anyway, what Emma knew could hardly harm him.

He drove on towards the city and after a while parked and went shopping. Within fifteen minutes he had acquired a pair of dark wide-framed sunglasses, a black straw hat and a blue light-weight sports coat with turned back cuffs and a flap on the breast pocket.

In this new outfit his appearance, if not radically altered, was nevertheless considerably different from the police description of him. With these clothes, the glasses to hide the peculiarly Anglo-Saxon blue of his eyes and his almost perfect Spanish, it was unlikely that anyone would take him for the wanted Englishman.

Altogether he felt considerably happier, lighter of heart, than he had for some time. He had done his best for Mr. Chatham, more in fact than had been asked and the rest of the job would soon be taken over by skilled professionals.

More, the problem of the photographs no longer bothered him so much. Short of a signed confession from the man who had put Josef up to taking them, certain people would never believe the whole thing had been faked. But Emma was not among them and neither, once he had heard the explanation, would be Mr. Chatham.

The only remaining difficulty, Paul thought, as he left the car in a side street and strolled down to the Gran Via, was the rape charge against him. But that, surely, was too preposterous to be insoluble. Once he had seen Conway and Allen he would get in touch with the Lady Wife and twist her arm a little. She'd see reason soon enough. He hoped.

He went into a restaurant for lunch. The disguise seemed to work. Nobody leapt up and yelled "Rapist!" Nobody, indeed, seemed to take any notice of him at all.

From the restaurant he went to Retiro Park and killed time sunbathing beside the lake and at a quarter to five he collected his car and drove to the Felix Hotel.

"Mr. Conway," he said. "He's expecting me."

The receptionist shrugged, regretfully. "He is not here, senor."

"Pardon?"

"He is not here."

"Mr. Allen then."

"He is not here, either."

Paul felt just the tiniest tug of panic. "But they were flying from London this afternoon. I had an appointment with them here at five o'clock."

"Si, senor. Unfortunately, the London plane was delayed. They have not arrived yet."

The little tug became a firm pull at Paul's guts. "When do you expect them?"

Another shrug. "I do not know, senor."

Sweating now, Paul went to the phone and called the airport. Yes, the plane had been delayed. A mechanical fault, quite unforeseeable, had developed just before the point of no return. By ill chance the aircraft had landed again at London Airport just too late for the passengers to transfer to the next flight out. Now there was no knowing quite when they would arrive but Paul could rest assured that everything possible was being done to get them to Madrid very, very soon.

Paul did not rest assured. The happiness of the early afternoon vanished and he was really scared now. Unless a miracle happened, he was on his own. A responsibility that had never been intended for him had become his.

And once again there was the question he seemed to have been asking himself for ever; what now?

A few minutes thought brought the answer, an answer anyway. He asked for writing paper and an envelope and when they came he wrote a brief account of everything that had happened since he got to Madrid and what he proposed to do and where he proposed to go that evening.

When it was finished he put it in the envelope and thought again. He could leave the message here to be given to Conway and Allen when they arrived. But they might not get it. It might be overlooked. It was unlikely but still possible and he could not afford to take chances.

He must entrust his report to somebody, hand it personally to someone who, he knew, would make sure that it got to Mr. Chatham's men as soon as they came in.

There was only one person he could trust to do that.

He drove to the Peniscola Hotel, adjusted his glasses, tipped his hat a little over his forehead, took a deep breath and strode boldly up to the plate glass doors. The porter held them wide and flashed the smooth, automatic grin of a man who expects to be tipped.

Paul made a big play of groping for change. As he had hoped, the man's eyes followed the movement of the hand. By the time twenty-five pesetas had changed pockets the porter was already poised to open the door for the next potential tipper. He had hardly glanced at Paul's face.

Unhurriedly, Paul crossed the foyer to the stairs. The police in the lounge stood out like navvies in a powder room. They were the shabby ones, the bored ones, the ones peeping furtively over their newspapers at all the comings and goings.

Emma's dear little sad man was slumped in an armchair beside the magazine kiosk, his hands resting listlessly on his thighs. He looked like a man who had been declared bankrupt on the same day as his house burned down and his wife ran away with his best friend.

The mournful eyes glanced up without curiosity as Paul passed, then fixed their attention on the door once more. Paul was in. Unchallenged.

He walked up to the second floor and made sure there were no more police loitering about in the corridors. Then he knocked on Emma's door.

She was wearing the same négligé she had worn the night before last and beneath it she had on what she had said she would have on at this time. No more. No less.

"Good God," she said. "I thought you were going to phone."

He pushed past her and closed the door. "I was." He leered amiably at her. "But when you told me what you were going to wear I couldn't keep away." He wasn't really in any mood for this kind of banter but it was better to wisecrack than think about the next few hours.

She backed warily into the bathroom. "I was only kidding. I mean, it wasn't an invitation. I ..." Quickly she slammed the door and locked it. Through the door, her voice muffled, she said: "Stay there and cool down. I won't be long."

"Don't forget the boots and the nurse's cap."

She came out again in a few minutes, wearing a white shirt and tight blue slacks and she looked no less desirable than she had before. It was unkind of fate, he thought, to deposit him so often in her bedroom at the wrong time and in the wrong circumstances.

She watched him quizzically as she busied around, pouring drinks.

"You seem to be taking a most awful risk in coming here," she said. "How did you get in?"

"I just strolled past all the bogeys downstairs. I saw your boy-friend, incidentally. A sad-looking case, isn't he?"

She nodded. "Rather sweet, though."

Paul put his glass down on the bedside table. "Did you find out what I wanted to know?"

"About Josef and Miguel? Yes. There was a special request from Huxter's office for them to take care of his guests."

"A written request?"

"Yes—signed by Huxter."

"I see." He took out his report and added to it what Emma had just told him. It was interesting, that was all. But whether it meant anything very significant was hard to tell at this stage.

"What are you doing?" she asked.

He stuck down the flap of the envelope and stared urgently into her wide, blue eyes. She gazed back, curious and guarded.

"Do something else for me, will you? Phone the Felix Hotel and ask for Mr. Conway or Mr. Allen."

"What ..."

"Please."

She shrugged and picked up the phone. When she was connected, she said: "May I speak to Mr. Conway or ... Oh, I see. Do you know when they'll be there? ... Thank you." She put the receiver down. "Not there."

Paul made a small, sad clucking sound with his tongue. It was getting on for seven now and he could no longer wait for Mr. Chatham's men.

"Look," he said. "This is very important. I want you to keep this envelope for me. Unopened. When I've gone I want you to call the Felix again and leave a message for Mr. Conway or Mr. Allen. Say you're speaking on behalf of Mr. Chatham's representative and you want Conway or Allen to call you as soon as they get in. It's very, very urgent."

He paused. She said: "Go on." A defensive smile lurked around her eyes and the edges of her mouth, as if she half suspected that this was some kind of a hoax.

"When they call, tell them to come round here—but don't let them in until you're sure of their identity. Then give them that envelope."

"It sounds awfully mysterious," she said. "Do tell me more."

"I can't," he said. "Honestly."

She lit a cigarette and sank gracefully into an arm-chair, letting one long, slim leg dangle over the side.

"I suppose," she said, "you'll be telling me next that you're a sort of secret agent, or something."

He hesitated. Then ... "Yes," he said. "I am. Something like that."

"Oh, for God's sake!" The blue eyes glinted humorously, but with just a touch of impatience, behind a veil of cigarette smoke.

"I'm not joking," he said.

She stared at him for a long moment, then she nodded, decisively. "All right. Tell me how Conway and Allen and I have to identify ourselves."

His heart sank. He had known it would come to this. If she hadn't taken him seriously before, how could she do so now when they had got down to the Boy Scout bit? He turned his back on her and looked out of the window.

"Well," he said, tonelessly, "You say 'Mr. Arthur sends his regards', and they say 'How kind of him. I hope he's well', and you say 'Yes, but his wife is ill'. Then they say 'I *am* sad. Nothing serious, I trust', and you say 'The usual trouble' That's all. Now please ..."

Behind him there was a muffled squeal of mirth. "You're marvellous," she said. "You almost had me believing you."

Swiftly, angrily, Paul turned and hit her hard across the face. The squeal of laughter turned into a little squeak of pain.

"Shut up," he said. "This isn't some merry little gag. I didn't come here to make you laugh. I'm leaving that envelope with you because you're the one person in Madrid I think I can trust and God knows I may be wrong. But I had to take the chance. Look ... if Conway and Allen don't get that message tonight, I may be killed. Is that funny? Are you still laughing?"

She put a hand to her cheek, stroking the place where he had hit her. Her eyes were no longer amused. There was worry in them now, and fear.

"I'm sorry," she murmured. "I'm very sorry."

Paul let out his breath in a long sigh of relief. "Thank God for that." He turned and went to the door.

She followed, caught him by the sleeve: "Paul …"

"Yes?"

Her fingers pressed gently into his arm. "Do take care," she said and kissed him, her body very close to his. A few breathless seconds later they broke away and Paul opened the door.

"Paul …"

"Yes?"

"What do you suppose is wrong with poor Mrs. Arthur?"

CHAPTER TWENTY-ONE

THE GO-BETWEEN

THE guard, lounging on the steps that led to the front door of Mandrake's villa, withdrew his left index finger from his right nostril and examined it with care.

He was bored. Not that picking his nose was a symptom of his boredom. He did that anyway. It was simply that he did it more often when he was bored.

He wondered how long the meeting inside the villa would go on. Not long, he hoped. The sooner it was over, the sooner he would be paid and free to go home to his wife and children in Barcelona. He had not seen them for three days, not since the English senor had moved in here with his strange young friend.

Still, the money was good; the work was easy. And it was not to be a long-term job. Tonight, in fact, it would end. The senor had told him so. Just as soon as the meeting was over he could collect his pay and go.

The guard had no idea who his employer was or what was going on inside the villa and he was not remotely curious about these matters. It was none of his business. So long as he was paid well and there was not much to do, why should he waste his time asking questions and interfering in things that did not concern him? Obviously, whatever the senor was up to could not be strictly legal, otherwise an armed guard would hardly have been necessary, but so what?

Better, he thought, not to think about these things. He liked to keep his nose clean, in more ways than one.

Thirty yards away a man appeared at the end of the drive and strolled towards him across the lawn.

The guard straightened up. Another one for the meeting, no doubt. "Good evening," he said, when the man was close to him.

"Good evening. I have an appointment with the senor. Is he in?"

"Si. The meeting has begun."

"Fine."

"You have no car, senor?"

"I left it at the gate," the man said. He stood still, listening. "What's that?"

"What?"

"A sound. Over there. I think there's someone in the bushes."

"Where, senor?" The guard turned in the direction from which, it seemed, the sound had come. And Paul Baker hit him very precisely and very hard behind the left ear with the handle of his automatic. The guard's knees bent like well-oiled hinges as he fell. For him the job was over. Rather sooner than he had expected.

Paul dragged the unconscious figure into the shrubbery, removed the man's gun and knife and left him. He threw the weapons deep into the bushes and, just as he had done that morning, crept round the side of the villa to where the water barrel stood beside the french windows.

All was much the same as it had been before. The longhaired boy was still there. So was Mandrake.

The main difference was that instead of Miguel the third man in the room was Big Bill Breugelhoffer.

Breugelhoffer. The funny little fat man with the impossible name. The man who had talked so solemnly about the sincerity of the preposterous film his employer was making. So this was the enemy. Good God Almighty!

The publicity man was sitting in the arm-chair which the long-haired boy had occupied that morning and Mandrake was opposite him on the settee. He had changed from sports clothes to a dark suit, white shirt, maroon tie and suede shoes. The more formal clothes suited him better, gave him back the dignity Paul remembered he had had during his political career.

The boy was lying on the floor reading a body culture magazine—the kind with straightforward, curiously unerotic, female nudes in the front and, catering for entirely different tastes, naked young men in high leather boots at the back. The long-haired boy was looking at the pictures at the back.

He still wore hipster pants and the pink shirt but he had added soft leather moccasins and a yellow pullover to his ensemble. The gold necklace was worn outside the pullover and hung down to his chest. His lips, which had appeared crimson that morning, now gleamed pink and moist and his eyelashes seemed thicker and blacker than they had been before. He showed no interest at all in the conversation around him.

Mandrake was saying: "Well, I can't wait any longer. I want to be away from here by ten-thirty. Let's get on with it." "Okay." Breugelhoffer took an envelope from his pocket and handed it across to the other man. "There's the proof that the final payment has been made. If you'd just like to hand over the film …"

Mandrake got up and went to the wall cabinet and opened the top drawer. He took out a small package and tossed it to Breugelhoffer. "Here."

"Thank you." Breugelhoffer stood up, loo, and there was an awkward silence. "Well," he said, at length. "I guess that's it then."

"Thank God for that," Mandrake said.

"Yessir, that's it." The silence hung around, reluctant to leave, as if neither man was sure how to bring the conversation to an end. "Well," Breugelhoffer said, "how about a little drink? A celebration. You know?"

"Oh, yes. Of course. How remiss of me. Paco," Mandrake said to the long-haired boy, "get some drinks will you. Scotch, I think."

The boy glanced up briefly from his magazine and looked with insolent eyes at the two men. Then he went on reading.

"Paco," Mandrake said, harshly. "You heard me. Get some drinks and be damn quick about it."

The boy stretched, took his time about getting up and slouched slowly from the room.

"That damn boy," Mandrake said. "I don't know why I put up with him."

Breugelhoffer's expression denoted polite sympathy and a certain degree of embarrassment. "Why don't you, ah, just throw him out?"

"Don't be naive," Mandrake said. "You know perfectly well why I don't."

"Yeah. Yeah, I guess so."

Mandrake took a cigar from a wooden box, bit the end off very neatly and lit it, holding the flame of the match carefully away from the leaf. "When he's not sulking, Paco can be very entertaining. I don't suppose you'd understand that, though."

"Well ..." To Breugelhoffer's obvious relief, Paco came back bearing a tray with whisky, glasses and ice. He poured two drinks, handed them to the men and flopped down on the floor again.

"Well," Breugelhoffer said. "I don't suppose we'll be meeting again."

"No, I don't suppose we will. There's no earthly reason why we should. I have nothing else to sell."

"Well, it's been nice doing business with you. Here's luck."

They raised their glasses to each other and finished their drinks quickly, each now eager to part company from the other. The deal was done. There was nothing more to be said. Mandrake was richer by two hundred thousand pounds or whatever his share was and soon Russia would be richer by the knowledge that the latest Anglo-American deterrent was a fiasco. Breugelhoffer put his glass down. "Well, good-bye then," he said.

Now Paul made his move.

To the occupants of the room it was as if he had simply materialised in the doorway—shot up through the ground or dropped from the roof. One second, it seemed, there was nobody within miles. The next, Paul was standing there, gun in hand, saying: "Just stay quite still, please."

The effect on Breugelhoffer was startling. He quivered and yelped, as if someone had jabbed him with something sharp, and whirled round with remarkable speed for one so stout. His mouth was open and the top set of his dentures had dropped grotesquely, so that he seemed to have two sets of teeth on his bottom gums.

Mandrake took the intrusion far more calmly. He stood quite still and surveyed Paul with round, bland eyes. "Well," he said, "you *are* a persistent young man."

Paco reacted hardly at all. He merely looked up from his reading, rolled over on his side, propped his head on his hand and looked on with more curiosity than anything else.

Paul came cautiously into the room, the gun pointing first at one then at each of the other occupants. "Throw that package towards me," he said to Breugelhoffer. "Gently, mind. If you do anything hasty I'm liable to shoot."

"With the safety catch on?" Mandrake enquired, mildly.

"The catch is off," Paul said, knowing it was.

Mandrake shrugged. "Oh, well. I saw it work in a film once. A very *bad* film I must confess."

Paul picked up the parcel without taking his eyes from the three people at the end of the gun. Now what?

He supposed he could shoot Mandrake and the others and walk out of the place but he rejected the idea, just as he had rejected it earlier that day. Or he could keep them here at gunpoint until Conway and Allen arrived—but that might mean waiting for hours. Or he could lock them in some room and run.

The third idea was the most attractive but the odds against him even getting out of the grounds before they were free and in pursuit were overwhelming. Unless there was a cellar in the place it was unlikely that the villa contained any room that was remotely escape-proof.

As if they realised his predicament, the others watched him expectantly. None of them spoke. The next move was up to him.

Paul backed over to the door that led into the hallway and kept his gun pointed at Mandrake. If this were a film, he thought, frowning in what he hoped was a menacing way at his captives, somebody about now would come through the door behind him and say: "All right, Baker. Drop that gun."

Somebody came through the door behind him and said: "All right, Baker. Drop that gun."

He had a momentary sense of nightmare, of utter disbelief. Then the gun dropped from his fingers and he turned, slowly, towards the newcomer.

Neddy Masters stood in the doorway, a new Neddy Masters who did not look at all like Cary Grant but looked, instead, hard and tough. A Neddy Masters with a small black revolver in his hand and a look in his eye that was distinctly unfriendly.

And with him was Emma Dane.

The sound Paul made, deep in his throat, was compounded equally of rage, self-contempt and despair.

He had gambled everything on this girl and he had lost. What he had thought to be a Queen had turned out to be the Joker in the pack—and in this game, it seemed, the Joker was wild.

His fingers, as he sprang towards her, curled into claws that grabbed avidly for the smooth, tanned softness of her throat.

He almost reached her. Then Neddy Masters' hand curved round in a short, swift arc and the gun barrel lashed across Paul's jaw, bringing with it a flash of agony and then total darkness.

CHAPTER TWENTY-TWO

PERSUASION

CONSCIOUSNESS came back slowly, like a weary traveller from a long way off. Sounds came first, soft, murmuring sounds that grew louder and louder until they were identifiable as voices. Mandrake's voice was chief among them.

"It's really quite simple. What Baker knows is not important. It's what his employers know that worries me."

"What the hell." This was Breugelhoffer. "You've got money and a good start. Nobody can touch you."

"That's not the point, is it?" Mandrake spoke with a sort of weary patience. "What I want to know is whether I can spend that money where I like or whether I shall have to go into hiding in South America or somewhere equally dreary and live like a recluse. It all depends on how much Baker told his employers."

"He couldn't have told them much," Breugelhoffer said.

"How do we know? We don't know when he last contacted them, or how long he's known who was involved. It's important to find these things out."

"Don't worry." Masters was speaking now. "They can't have any proof whatever he told them. I suggest we shoot him and get out."

"Oh, do shut up," said Mandrake. "All you think about is killing people. You really are a broken reed when it comes to emergencies."

Paul opened his eyes. The light hurt and he closed them again, quickly. But he had seen enough.

So the place did have a cellar. And he was in it. Tied to a chair. Cautiously he tested the bonds on his wrists. With a mighty bound, he thought, our hero was free.

The bonds refused to snap, refused even to slacken. So much for that theory. He opened his eyes again.

There was a window high up in the wall but hardly big enough for a man to crawl through, even if he could reach it. There was a door, too, but it was shut and bolted and Mandrake and Breugelhoffer were between him and it, which ruled it out as a way of escape since he could hardly hope to hunk himself and the chair over there without anyone noticing.

Besides, Masters was standing alongside him and he still had the revolver in his hand.

Paul made an involuntary movement of his head and groaned aloud as a streak of pain seared through it.

"Aha," Mandrake said. "He's awake."

Paul squinted up at him. Mandrake and Breugelhoffer came over to him but Masters merely glanced up briefly and gave him an amiable nod.

"Did you hear what we were saying?" Mandrake asked.

"Enough."

"Good. Well, then, how much *did* you tell the Department?"

"I've nothing to say."

"Look, old chap, be reasonable. You've nothing to gain by being stubborn. I know we're only amateurs, really, but we can be very persuasive. Masters, show him how persuasive we can be."

"Righto," Masters said and hit Paul savagely on the cheek with his gun barrel.

The pain was indescribable. To Paul it seemed that his jaw must have splintered, that half his teeth had come out. His mouth filled with blood that leaked through his lips and trickled down his chin.

"Again?" Masters asked.

"Not yet." Mandrake smiled his winning politician's smile, as if he were seeking Paul's vote at a by-election. "Do be sensible. Masters' methods, crude though they are, worked very well with Neece and your friend Blake. They're bound to work with you, too, in the end."

Masters gave Paul a friendly wink. "Better do as he says, old boy."

"You," Paul said, his voice thick with pain. "My friend. My old mate."

Masters said: "Nothing personal in this, you know. Be much nicer if we could settle the whole thing on an amicable basis."

"I don't understand you. Why are you doing this?" Paul was trying to gain time, though to what end he had no idea.

"Question of money, isn't it?" Masters said. "I mean, as a PRO I get two thousand a year and a few quid fiddled from my exes. Chicken feed, you see. Take me years to save a decent sum on that kind of income. But after this little job … well, I shall simply retire. In luxury, too. Thanks to Big Bill, of course. He put me up to it. He's the pro."

"Pro? You mean a spy?"

"No, no," Breugelhoffer said. "Merely a businessman. I find someone with something to sell and someone else who wants to buy it and I negotiate the deal for them. I'm not a secret agent, I'm a commercial agent. Well, a secret commercial agent, if you like …"

"And a killer," Paul said, "don't forget that."

"Well … I try to avoid violence but I'm afraid this time it became inevitable. But you understand, *I* didn't actually kill anybody."

"No." Paul looked at Masters. "You did that, didn't you?"

"Can't make omelets without breaking eggs, old boy."

Paul shook his head. "Don't you care?"

"Not really," Masters said, indifferently. "I thought I would but I don't. Killing's quite easy, actually."

Mandrake broke in. "Let's get this matter finished. For the last time, Mr. Baker, how much did you tell your Department?"

Paul said nothing and the quiet hovered around the room. Mandrake said: "Very well. Masters."

Masters stepped forward again, took a handful of Paul's hair, tugged his head back almost gently, and hit him again with the gun barrel.

Now Paul's whole face was just one area of agony, a centre of pain in which there were no thoughts, only sensations, so acute as to be unbearable.

Vaguely, he heard Breugelhoffer moaning: "Not on the face. I can't stand blood," and Mandrake's sharp command: "The body, Masters. Concentrate on the body."

And then the pain shifted to his shoulders and chest, to his ribs and stomach, to his thighs, to his shins and his ankles as the pistol-whipping went on.

Suddenly, it stopped.

Masters said: "He's tougher than I thought. Let's see how he likes it on the cobblers."

But he never did find out. For, as Masters drew his arm back and sighted on the target, the accumulated punishment Paul had suffered took its effect and he fainted.

Again it was the sounds, of movements and voices, that came through first. Then there was the chill shock of cold water, being splashed vigorously into his face and he blinked and looked up.

Nothing had changed. The three of them were still there. Mandrake making clicking sounds of impatience with his teeth; Breugelhoffer looking sick at the sight of Paul's bruised, cut face; Masters massaging his wrist as if it ached a little.

The pain was still there, too, but in a curious way, Paul seemed to have grown used to it. It was like a part of his life and the time when he was free of it was almost beyond recall, forever ago.

"There's no more time to be lost," Mandrake said, testily. "We can't prolong this nasty business just for Masters' satisfaction. Bring the girl in."

Breugelhoffer left the room and nobody said anything until he came back. Emma was with him.

Her hands were tied in front of her, one wrist crossed over the other. Her dress was ripped from shoulder to waistline and there was a bruise on her jaw where somebody had hit her. The stains where tears had dried showed plainly on her cheeks.

Paul stared at her, in bewilderment first then, as understanding crept in on him, with a strange, illogical relief.

When she had appeared earlier with Masters, he had assumed that she had betrayed him; that she was with Mandrake and the others. For them. Against him. An enemy.

But he had been wrong. She was a prisoner, just as he was. And now as Breugelhoffer pushed her into the room, Paul felt something almost like joy. She had not betrayed him at all. Thank God for that. She had not betrayed him at all.

Masters said: "Surprised to see her? Thought you might be. I saw you leaving her room tonight and guessed you'd probably cooked something up between you. So I dropped in on her a bit later and told her you were in trouble and needed her. Worked like a dream, old boy. Must have touched the mother instinct in her."

Emma glanced across at Paul. "Sorry," she said.

He closed one eye in a painful wink. "Don't worry." His voice was thick, mumbling, as if his tongue and lips were too fat for the rest of his mouth.

Mandrake said smoothly: "But she should worry. Because, you see, I'm going to set Masters on her. You leave me no alternative. You're being silly and stubborn so I shall just have to see whether Miss Dane can't be persuaded to cooperate." He nodded towards Masters but Masters stayed where he was, frowning uncertainly.

"I don't like this," he said. "I mean, picking on women. It doesn't seem right."

The light was shining on one side of his face, the other being partly in shadow, and there was a distinctly noble air about him. Paul had never seen him looking quite so magnificently like Cary Grant in his life.

Mandrake said: "For God's sake, man, this is no time to start having scruples. These two are as much a menace to you as they are to me. Get on with it."

"Why don't you do it?" Masters asked.

"Because it's your job. You said you didn't mind doing this kind of thing. So get on. The more quickly we dispose of this pair, the more quickly you become rich."

Masters thought about it. "Well, all right," he said grudgingly. He went over to Emma. "I really am sorry about this," he said and drew back the revolver. And stopped.

"I can't do it," he said, sullenly. "Not to a woman."

There was a sound from Mandrake, inarticulate, hysterical. He moved, pounced, across the room and snatched the gun from Masters' hand. "Give it to me, you bloody fool!" he said, screamed almost. "I'll do it."

Paul struggled pointlessly against the ropes that held his hands and feet. Emma was biting her lip and staring up at Mandrake. The panic in her face was clear enough.

"Leave her alone," Paul said. He was beaten and he knew it. They all knew it. "You wasted your time bringing her here. She knows nothing. I came to help Blake but … we didn't get together until it was too late."

Mandrake dropped the gun and stood with a hand over his eyes. The fury of a moment ago was draining visibly from him. Not that it mattered. The seed of it was still there, would always be there, and rage would swiftly flare again if further frustrations were offered him.

"What about this?" He held up the envelope in which Paul had put his report. "Who was it for?"

"The Department sent two men over. They were delayed. That's why I came here tonight." Paul's voice was empty. If Emma had been unable to contact Conway and Allen, he was truly beaten. This was one time when the cavalry wouldn't arrive to save the wagon train. This was the picture where the evil Redskins rode happily off into the sunset.

"Does the Department know what's in this report?"

Paul shook his head.

"So they still have no proof—even about my part in all this?" Mandrake bent over him, watching his face carefully

"I haven't given them any. They know what you're doing, why you're here but they can't prove anything."

Mandrake smiled. "Well, at last. You could have saved everyone a lot of bother if you'd told me all this earlier. Still … the only thing that remains is what to do with you. You'll have to die, you understand."

"Her as well?"

"I'm afraid so. It's regrettable but there you are. You're to blame, you know. You should never have involved her."

"But ..."

Mandrake shook his head decisively. "There's no point in arguing. You can't possibly talk me out of it for the simple reason that you have nothing to bargain with."

He turned to Breugelhoffer, now happily recovered from the ordeal of watching Paul bleed.

"It will have to look like a quarrel, I think. A fight over the girl. Shots fired all round. Death on every hand. Not very good, I'm afraid, but it should work." He paused. "Would you mind doing it?"

Breugelhoffer frowned. "I suppose not. There's no real alternative, is there?"

Slowly, he bent and picked up the revolver from the floor where Mandrake had dropped it. He cocked it and aimed it first at Paul, then at Emma. His finger tightened on the trigger and Paul shut his eyes and prayed to the God he had neglected far too often all his life.

The moment passed. Breugelhoffer swivelled the gun round until it pointed at Neddy Masters. "Him first?"

"Why not?" said Mandrake.

Masters stared at them. There was an idiotic grin on his lips. "Cut it out, old boy," he said. "I'm on your side, remember? Don't play the fool. It's Baker you have to kill, not me, old boy. Not me."

The gun jumped in Breugelhoffer's hand. The sound of the explosion ricocheted off the walls. A hole appeared neatly between Masters' eyes and he fell, as relaxed as only the dead can be, onto the concrete floor. Breugelhoffer glanced away so as not to be offended by the blood.

"Well done," Mandrake said.

"Thank you. He was right, you know. It's really quite easy."

"You'd better kill the others with Baker's gun," Mandrake said. "It's going to be a pretty wild sort of situation anyway. We don't want to add to the confusion by killing them all with the same weapon."

"Good thinking." Breugelhoffer reached into his pocket and brought out Paul's little automatic.

From outside came the sound of a car starting up, the engine revving frantically. Mandrake and Breugelhoffer gazed, startled, at each other. Then …

"It's that boy," Mandrake yelled. "He's taking the car! We must stop him."

He rushed to the door, fumbling with the bolt. "There's another car," Breugelhoffer said. "It doesn't matter."

"He's going, don't you see? He's leaving. I've got to stop him. For God's sake, come on!"

Breugelhoffer hesitated, looking at Paul and Emma. Then he shrugged and followed Mandrake out. The door closed behind him and the key turned with a harsh, final sound in the lock.

CHAPTER TWENTY-THREE
DEATH IN THE PROPS DEPARTMENT

"ARE they going to kill us?" Emma asked.

"What?" Paul pushed aside the thoughts that whirled about in his mind and turned his attention to the girl.

The panic had gone from her eyes but her voice was hushed and scared. The point of breakdown into hysteria was not far away.

"Are they going to kill us?" she asked again.

"No, of course not," Paul said, with considerably more assurance than he felt. "Why should they?"

She gestured towards the body of Masters. "They killed him. Paul, I don't understand. Why did they kill him?"

"God knows. I've no idea."

He could guess, though. Masters had been an amateur while Mandrake and Breugelhoffer were both, in their different ways, professionals. Masters had been picked to do a certain job, to do, in fact, the rougher stuff for which his two colleagues had little taste and no real aptitude. Breugelhoffer had chosen him, almost certainly after a very careful study of his subject and a long precise sounding-out period in which, no doubt, Masters' greed and indifference to human life and pain—other people's pain—had emerged and shown him excellently suited to the task in hand.

But now the deal was closed. The job for which Masters had been hired was finished. At this stage he became a menace to his colleagues. Because he was an amateur, because, indeed, he was the kind of man he was, he would have spent his money unwisely, ostentatiously, and thus drawn attention to himself. Neither Breugelhoffer nor Mandrake would have wished to chance that.

They were both, by the nature of their callings—the commercial agent dealing in classified information, and the politician—accustomed to picking their way through minefields; patient men who knew when to bide their time. Masters did not. He was impulsive, and one ill-considered move by him could have meant danger to them all. And so, because he was expendable anyway and must have been considered so from the start, he was eliminated. Now, as far as the authorities were concerned, he was merely one side of what was going to look like a very ill-fated eternal triangle.

For, clearly, whenever his body was discovered, the bodies of Paul and Emma would be keeping it company.

"What shall we do?" Emma asked.

Paul looked at her hands. They were bound tightly at the wrists but her fingers were free. "Try to untie me, will you?"

She knelt beside him and began to pick at the ropes on his wrists. "Have they gone away?" she asked. "Do you think they've left us?"

"Maybe." Little chance of that, though. Once Mandrake had sorted out the business of Paco, they would be back and then it would soon be over. We are, Paul thought, about fifteen minutes away from death. He stopped thinking about it although, oddly enough, he was not afraid. It was too impossible to believe.

"Hurry up," he said.

"I'm being as quick as I can. It's not easy." She sounded on the point of tears. But her fingers plucked faster at the knots and in a moment Paul's hands were free.

"Good girl." She stood in front of him while he worked at the cords on her wrists. "What happened to you?"

"It was like Masters said. He came into my room and said you were in trouble and wanted to see me. Like a fool I believed him. I'm sorry."

"I'm sorry, too. When I saw you with him, I thought ..."

"I know you did. That was silly of you."

"I'll make it up to you, though." Oh, sure. How? He said: "What happened to that guard they had upstairs?"

"He came in just after Masters knocked you out. Breugelhoffer gave him some money and told him to go away. I suppose he went ... Paul, what's this all about? I know that other man is Henry Mandrake because I recognised him, but what on earth is going on?"

"One day," he said, "maybe I'll be able to tell you."

The cord fell from her wrists and she rubbed the places where the thin material had dug into her flesh. Paul thought about the things she had told him.

With the guard gone and Masters dead there were only Mandrake, Breugelhoffer and perhaps Paco to deal with. Put like that it did not seem too difficult, except for the little matter of precisely how to deal with them. Certainly they expected no trouble, or they would hardly have left him and Emma alone, and indeed why should they? They were armed and he was not. It was as simple as that. What he needed was a gun.

He bent down to untie the ropes around his ankles and something hard pressed into the base of his stomach.

For a second he could hardly believe his luck. The little automatic in its crazily-situated holster—they had missed it! It was still there, tucked snugly into his crotch.

Frantically, he pulled at his zip and was plunging his hand into his trousers when Emma turned towards him.

"What the hell are you doing!" she said.

"Getting my gun out."

"What!" She reached a high C of disbelief.

"Oh, for Pete's sake. This. Look." He took the tiny automatic from its pouch and showed it to her.

"Well," she said, after a long pause. "That's a relief."

Stiffly, he got up. He still found it hard to speak clearly and his face and body hurt a lot but at least he could move about without too much discomfort. He said: "Listen, when they come back I want you to keep well away from me. There's going to be some shooting and ..."

"Look out," she said. "They're coming now."

"Get over there—away from the door."

The key turned in the lock and they heard Breugelhoffer saying: "Don't worry about him. He'll be too scared to go to the police."

"It's not that," Mandrake said. "I just don't like him leaving me. I wish we'd been able to stop him."

"Hell, there are plenty of boys like that in the world. You're well rid of him."

"You don't understand," Mandrake said. "It's no good talking about it. You just don't understand."

They came into the room, Breugelhoffer first with Paul's other automatic in his hand.

"Well," Mandrake said. "You're free. I thought you might be. Have you said tender farewells to each other?"

"We need more time. There's such a lot to say." Paul watched Breugelhoffer, waiting for the moment when the man would take his eyes off him.

Mandrake chuckled, good humour suddenly restored. "Unfortunately, time is the one commodity you're short of."

From across the room, Emma said, in a scared little voice. "You're not going to kill us?"

For a fraction of a second Breugelhoffer looked towards her and in that tiny section of time Paul brought up his pistol and fired. The bullet that had been aimed hastily at Breugelhoffer's heart embedded itself in his wrist. He gave a sharp moan and the gun fell from his hand.

"Christ!" Mandrake said. "He's got a gun. You bloody fool! He's got a gun."

Breugelhoffer clutched his wounded hand against his chest. His face was grey and frightened. "I'm bleeding," he said. "I'm bleeding."

"The gun," Mandrake said. "Where did you get the gun?"

Paul patted the front of his trousers with his free hand. "It was there all the time."

Mandrake grabbed Breugelhoffer by the shoulder and shook him. "You fool! You said you'd searched him."

"I did ... Oh, God, I need help—look at the blood. I ... How was I to know he kept a pistol in his jock strap?"

Mandrake said: "You bloody idiot!" and with a suddenness that took them all by surprise, he hurled Breugelhoffer against Paul. Instinctively, Paul fired. The bullet squelched into the fat body and then the two of them tumbled to the floor. The door slammed shut as Mandrake rushed from the room.

Paul pushed the dead weight of Breugelhoffer away from him. "Wait here," he said to Emma, and then he was off in pursuit of Mandrake.

There was a corridor outside the cellar and a flight of stairs leading up to the main part of the house. He took them two and three at a time and emerged into a square entrance hall. Now which way?

A sound from his left. He whirled, found himself looking into the room with the french windows. Mandrake stood by the desk, the packet with the roll of microfilm in one hand, a pistol in the other.

The two men saw each other simultaneously; fired simultaneously; missed. Then Mandrake was at the french windows, through them, and racing across the lawn towards the shrubbery at the back of the garden.

At the terrace Paul took quick aim and fired again. The bullet passed over Mandrake's head and flew off into the night. And Mandrake was gone, crashing his way through the bushes towards the fence between the villa's garden and the grounds of the palace where Huxter's unit worked by day.

Paul went after him, letting the noise of the man's progress guide him. Branches whipped his aching face. Thorns clutched like tiny grasping hands at his clothes.

The bushes ended. Ahead was a stretch of uneven ground and beyond it the fence. Mandrake was almost there.

As Paul came into the open, Mandrake fired—a wild shot that screamed into the bushes, far off to Paul's right.

Panting, the air burning his lungs and throat. Paul ran on, stumbling as his feet caught in the rough, wiry grass. With a leap, he grasped the top of the fence and was over it in time to see Mandrake heading for the plaster wall of Huxter's temple. Another shot—and this time the bullet spat up earth at Paul's feet. Paul's answering shot flaked paint off the temple wall.

Now Mandrake was through the balsa wood doors, slamming them behind him. Paul followed, hit the doors with his shoulder, tearing them away from their flimsy hinges.

Ahead was the huge old barn that Huxter's unit used as the property department. And Mandrake was inside it. He had to be. There was nowhere else he could have gone.

With a disregard for his own safety that amazed him, Paul raced to the door of the barn, kicked it open and plunged into the darkness inside. A bullet shrilled past his head and he threw himself to the floor, rolling over until he reached the cover of a pile of saddles in the corner.

Now there was stillness, the only sounds the wheezing of his breath and the pumping of his heart.

He lay motionless, gazing around, trying to pinpoint Mandrake's position.

The place had changed since the day of his fight with the bearded actor. Then it had been practically empty—now it was full of stuff, the props and costumes handed in by the extras at the end of the day's work.

Armour and the trappings of horses lay in heaps about the floor. Roman togas, slave-girl costumes, tunics, hung from the walls like the wardrobe for some gigantic fancy dress ball. Overhead, about ten feet from the floor, a wide balcony ran round the sides of the room, reached by a flight of stairs near the door. In neat piles along the balcony were the spears and swords and shields of Huxter's Roman army.

Of Mandrake there was no sign.

Paul began to edge round the room, keeping to the cover of the bundles that littered the floor.

Behind him, the door creaked suddenly. He half rose, turned towards it—and from across the room Mandrake fired. Paul twisted round swiftly. There was a rustling on the stairs—a footstep? a rat?—and a movement beyond the stairs. He aimed towards the movement and pulled the trigger. From a little to the left of where he had aimed another shot cracked back at him and the hot breath of the bullet passed terrifyingly close to his face.

Paul flung himself down behind a heap of metal breastplates beneath the overhanging balcony. His head ached relentlessly and fear was tying a knot in his insides. There was just one shot left in the little gun.

And Mandrake knew it.

For now, from the darkness, he spoke; his voice as calm and smooth as ever; the voice of a man who saw victory ahead.

"Mr. Baker," he said, "unless I have miscalculated you are very nearly out of ammunition. One bullet left, I believe. Be careful how you use it."

Paul lay flat on the ground, peering round the armour, trying to place where the voice had come from.

Mandrake said: "I have three bullets. That makes me a three-to-one favourite, I think."

Still Paul said nothing. His outstretched arm was flat against the floor, his chin resting against his bicep as he squinted along his arm to the sights of the gun. He waited.

"I don't want to kill you," Mandrake said. "Can't we come to some arrangement? A financial arrangement. After all, we surely have nothing against each other personally."

The voice seemed to come from behind a great heap of horse blankets against the far wall. But Mandrake himself was well-hidden. Coax him out, Paul told himself. Keep him talking.

"You're a traitor," he said.

"From necessity, Mr. Baker, not from choice. You must realise that. My position was taken from me, my reputation was ruined. I had no alternative."

"It was your own fault. Nobody's to blame but you." Paul's mind was only half on what he was saying. His eyes searched the blackness around the blankets. Still no movement.

"Because I'm a homosexual—is that what you mean? A barbaric judgement, don't you think? They persecuted me. It was a witch-hunt, don't you see?"

Again that scurrying along the balcony. Rats. It must be—hundreds of them probably. Paul squirmed at the thought.

"You weren't persecuted," he said. "You know why they arrested you. Because you were a security risk."

Show yourself, damn you.

Mandrake's sigh, a sound full of resignation, of despair at the futility of arguing with those who will not listen, floated across the room. "That's very glib, Mr. Baker. Tell me, will you, why a man like me should be a worse security risk than a man like you?"

Was that a movement—that brief flicker across the room? It was too late anyway. The moment had gone.

Paul said: "Blackmail." He suspected that he was being glib again.

"Oh, dear. Don't you think people have tried to blackmail me? And don't you think I know how to handle them? Without turning traitor, as you put it, to do so?"

Paul eased his cramped limbs into a more comfortable position. He was tense, edgy with waiting and watching.

"You asked for it," he said. "You must have known the risk when you joined that fairy club."

"That was unwise, I admit that," Mandrake said. "But we were all … what's the phrase … consenting adults. Nobody was seduced or raped. We didn't corrupt any little boys."

God, why doesn't he move, Paul thought.

Again, there was the rustling above and this time Mandrake seemed to hear it, too, for now, at last, there was a quick movement across the room as the man turned, involuntarily, towards the sound. Just for a moment his shape showed, blurred, above the blankets and Paul fired his last shot.

The crash of the gun echoed back from the walls, slow to die away. Smoke hung, pungent, on the air. For a while nothing stirred.

Then Mandrake came out from behind the blankets and advanced into the centre of the room.

"Unless you have yet another revolver concealed in your underpants, I rather fear you're out of ammunition." There was a note of quiet and totally anticipated triumph in his voice.

Silently Paul cursed his own rashness. Why had he not waited, taken aim? Why had he blazed away like some hero in a Western, predestined by the script to come out on top?

Mandrake laughed. "Come out. Preferably with your hands up but come out anyway."

"Go to Hell," Paul said, feebly.

With a few quick steps Mandrake was beside him, looming dark and menacing in the gloom of the place. "I'm sorry it had to come to this," he said. "We could have made an arrangement, you know. I wouldn't have double-crossed you."

Paul's gaze fastened on the gun in the man's hand. "For heaven's sake," he said. "Get it over with."

Mandrake's hand came up slowly until the muzzle was aimed at a spot in the centre of Paul's forehead. With a hideous fascination Paul saw the knuckle turn white as the index finger tightened on the trigger.

"Don't move," Mandrake said. "The least I can give you is a quick death."

And then, almost too late, Paul understood the meaning of the sounds he had heard, the creaking of the door, the rustlings on the stairs and the balcony.

Lithe and graceful, like an Olympic diver, Emma Dane launched herself from the balcony above them and the spear she held before her, clenched fiercely in her slim hands, took Mandrake in the throat as he glanced up. The shot he fired flew into the rafters and then he was down, the velocity of Emma's fall and the weight of her body driving the spear through him and into the wooden floorboards.

A choking, gurgling sound like the last cry of a drowning kitten came from him and then he was still.

CHAPTER TWENTY-FOUR

CALL OFF THE POLICE

THEY got back to the hotel soon after three o'clock and went in by way of the fire escape to avoid any policemen who might still be waiting in the lobby. Neither of them had spoken during the drive through the sleeping city.

From the barn to which Emma had been led by the sound of shooting, they had gone back to the villa to retrieve Paul's other automatic. There he burned the microfilm, which he had taken from Mandrake's body, and cleared up all traces of his own and Emma's presence.

Soon, later today perhaps, the bodies would be found and the police would have the unenviable task of working out exactly what happened and who had done what and with which and to whom. Paul doubted strongly that they would ever manage it.

Now he and Emma stood together in the corridor on the second floor of the hotel. She looked exhausted, drained of anything but an overwhelming desire to sleep.

"All right?" he asked. She nodded, even managed something pretty close to a smile.

"Go on to your room," he said. "Have you got the key?"

"It's in my handbag."

"Off you go, then."

"What about you?"

"There's something I want to clear up."

When she had gone, he went to Huxter's suite and knocked. After he had knocked twice more the door opened and Huxter stood there, puffy with sleep and ludicrous in a scarlet kimono with a black sash that made him look like some old judo expert gone to seed.

"You!" he said. His eyes were huge with surprise. "Christ, you got a nerve …"

"I want to see your wife," Paul said.

"The hell you do! I'm gonna call the police."

The Lady Wife appeared behind her husband. The kimono she wore matched Huxter's but did a lot more for her than his did for him. "Well, well, well," she murmured. "Baker the raper."

Paul said, calmly: "I'm trying to tell your husband how foolish he would be to call the police but he's a very pig-headed man and I'm not getting very far."

"Go back to bed, honey," Huxter growled. "I'll handle this guy."

"Be quiet."

To Paul: "Why shouldn't he call the police?"

"Let me in and I'll explain."

"To him?" Her eyes were hard, calculating.

"To you."

She thought about it. "All right."

"But listen …" Huxter turned to her but she was walking away, back into the bedroom and, while her husband hesitated, Paul went in after her.

"Go out on the balcony," she said to Huxter. "The fresh air will do you good."

"But honey … it's cold out there, for Chrissakes. A man could get pneumonia."

"Go out on the balcony." She spoke as a mother addressing a stubborn child. He looked at her beseechingly but there was no softening in her expression. He glared at Paul and stamped sulkily out into the cool night air, hugging his absurd kimono to him in a wholly unsuccessful attempt at dignity.

The Lady Wife closed the windows and drew the net curtains together. "Well," she said. "What do you want to say?"

Paul flopped into a chair. His head and body ached abominably and he felt exhausted. "Tell him to call off the police."

She perched on the arm of a chair and lit a cigarette. One long white leg showed clear to the thigh as the kimono fell open. "Why?"

"For God's sake," Paul said, "you know why. If he insists on having me arrested I'll have to tell him some things about you—your former profession to start with. That should get his interest."

She blew a smoke ring and put an index finger neatly through the centre of it. "He knows already."

"All right." Paul had realised this was a possibility. "Does he know about you coming to my room that morning? Or about the actor and the 'fee' you paid him to beat me up? Or about Grainger being in your room when I was supposed to be raping you?"

She smiled. "Do you think he'd believe any of it? Those are the kind of stories he'd expect you to make up."

"Okay then," Paul said. "How about this? I get arrested and I'm charged with rape and instead of telling these things to your husband, I tell them in court—with that actor and Grainger as witnesses."

He leaned over and took the cigarette from her fingers. The lipstick she had left on the end made the smoke taste sweet in his mouth.

"The point is," he went on, "that whether I was acquitted or not there'd be so much muck thrown at you that maybe a little of it would stick. Enough, perhaps, for old J.J. to start wondering.

With a man like that a little suspicion could go a long way. The next step might be a private detective watching you. And then ..."

Huxter's baleful face appeared at the window, seen dimly behind the net curtains. "Can't I come in now? I'm freezing to death out here."

With an abstracted gesture she waved him away. Then she said: "You may just have a point. In any event, I don't want to take any more risks than I have to. When I get divorced it'll be on *my* terms. All right, then. Between you and me I don't think I intended the game to go much further than this anyway."

Paul got up and went over to her. "You're a hell of a woman," he said.

"You keep going up in my estimation, too. Come and see me when we get back to London."

"Yes. Perhaps."

"Perhaps?" She raised one eyebrow. "We'll see about that."

She paused, one hand on the window catch ready to open it. "What happened to your face? A woman?"

"You might say that. There was a woman involved."

"Mmm. I like rough games myself."

Imperiously she gestured to her husband to come in. When he had done so, she said: "Darling, there's been a little misunderstanding. You must drop the charges against Mr. Baker. He's explained the whole thing."

"The hell he has!" said Huxter. "Now, see here ..."

"Baby." She put her arms around him and winked at Paul over her husband's shoulder. "It's all right, really it is. Now be a darling and phone the desk downstairs and tell them to let Mr. Baker have his room back."

"Listen to me ..." But she cut him short by kissing him on the mouth and saying softly: "Do it now, baby, so we can go back to bed, hmm?"

With her left hand she stroked the back of Huxter's neck; with her right she gestured to Paul to go.

He waved goodbye, wondering what kind of a story she would cook up for her husband. He had no doubt she would make it plausible.

She blew Paul a kiss and silently her lips formed the words: "See you in London ..."

CHAPTER TWENTY-FIVE

AND SO TO BED

T HE waiter who showed him to his room was a new man, one Paul had never seen before.

"What happened to Miguel and Josef?" he asked.

"They have gone, senor. Nobody knows what happened to them."

That meant three of them, Miguel, Paco and the villa guard, were still free. Well, so what? They were unimportant, fringemen who probably knew nothing of what was really involved in Mandrake's dealings with Breugelhoffer and Masters. The hell with it, let them go.

The bed was soft and soothing to Paul's aching body and sleep, rather to his surprise, came at once. It didn't last long, though. At ten o'clock the call he had booked to Mr. Chatham came through and at the same time the waiter arrived with morning tea.

Drowsily Paul yelled "Come in" to the waiter and sat up to reach for the phone. He was stiff and sore all over but his reflection, glimpsed in the wall mirror, did not look as bad as he had expected.

"Baker here," he said.

"Identify yourself." The dry, distant voice was unmistakable.

They had their little chat about Mr. and Mrs. Arthur.

"Right. Report, please." Mr. Chatham did not believe in wasting words on the telephone, particularly on an open line. In such circumstances reports had to be delivered and commented upon in a kind of shorthand.

Paul said: "It worked out okay. The deal fell through."

"I see. Who stopped it?"

"I did."

"I see," Mr. Chatham said again. "And our rivals?"

"There were three of them involved. The one we knew about and two others. They've all left. Permanently. I sent them away."

"That won't cause you any inconvenience with the authorities, I trust."

"I don't think so."

There was a pause. Mr. Chatham said: "I've received a remarkable photograph …"

"Destroy it. Please," Paul said, hurriedly. "It was a mistake."

"Yes. Nevertheless, I should like an explanation when you return here." A deep sigh drifted along the wire from Mr. Chatham's end. "I imagine you haven't spoken to Mr. Conway or Mr. Allen."

"No. They arrived rather too late. Why?"

"I cabled them a message last night. They were supposed to pass it on to you, too."

Again a pause. Paul waited hungrily for some word of praise, something a little warm to contrast with Mr. Chatham's cold, formal Civil Service manner; something to offset the sick feeling of despondency that asserted itself whenever Paul thought of the things he had had to do.

He asked: "Is everything all right?"

"Not entirely." Mr. Chatham coughed gently. "Have you got the newspapers there?"

Paul was alarmed. Was it something the police had discovered? Something about Blake? Mandrake? A mistake Paul had made that would land him straight back into trouble? He reached for the papers which the waiter had brought with the tea. "Only the Spanish ones," he said. "The London papers haven't got here yet."

"I think," Mr. Chatham said, "that you'll find the item I mean on the overseas page. It's quite an interesting one. Most papers should be carrying it."

Paul turned over the pages and the story leapt out and hit him. It was an inside page lead with a London dateline and the headline translated roughly into "Atom Ships Fiasco". The story beneath said: "A secret Anglo-American plan to build a fleet of atom-powered battleships was revealed in London last night— and admitted at once to be a failure.

"The news was given at a Press conference called by Mr. Howard Goodenough, the British Minister of Forward Planning. Britain and America, he said, had spent more than 400 million pounds on trying to develop a fleet of small, deadly, atom-powered warships.

"But the project had now been abandoned because the cost would be out of all proportion to the effectiveness of the vessels …"

Paul said: "Christ! What are they …"

"There was a change of plan." Mr. Chatham interrupted him smoothly, before he could say too much. Indiscretions on an open line were positively not to be encouraged. "The Other Side was becoming too worried. Their people, of course, believed the plan to be feasible and, as a counter-measure, to protect their own interests, they had started conferring—far too closely for our comfort—with their Far East associates.

"So it was decided, on the highest possible authority, to make the statement you have just read. The news was announced simultaneously in Britain and America. As you may have guessed, the message I sent to Conway and Allen was to suspend operations—or rather, to observe but not to act."

Paul thought of the events of the last few days. Of the men and the girl who had died. Of Emma Dane and the guilt and grief and horror she had felt, and would never quite forget, when she looked down on that body with the spear in its throat.

"So it was all a waste," he said, dully. "Everything that happened—it was all a waste."

"In a manner of speaking," Mr. Chatham said. "No blame attaches to you, of course. In other circumstances, it would have been considered that you had done rather well." He cleared his throat. "Incidentally, what happened to that microfilm?"

"I destroyed it."

"Pity. We'll have to get another roll taken."

"What?"

"Well, you know what it's like in this business … No, perhaps you don't. Neither side believes anything that's put out in official statements. Proof is demanded. So we'll have to take some more film and leak it to one of their people. That should ease the situation …"

Paul put the phone down. For several minutes he sat, hunched in the bed, staring at the wall opposite, not really seeing it, not seeing anything and not feeling anything either, just letting the memories stab through his mind like sharp little blades.

He was still sitting like that when the phone rang and Emma said: "Paul? Do you remember once I said that when I wanted you to come to my room I'd let you know?"

"Yes," he said. "I remember." His voice was as bleak as hers.

"Well, would you come now? I need comforting. I need it very, very badly."

"So do I," he said. "So do I."

www.ingramcontent.com/pod-product-compliance
Lightning Source LLC
Chambersburg PA
CBHW071430260626
47170CB00008B/2663

* 9 7 8 1 9 5 4 8 4 1 9 6 3 *